Black; nothing but black. And no response when he whispered, "Scotty, hey, Scotty!" as loud as he dared.

Christ, the kid probably fell or something, he decided, and made his way along the wall to the lefthand fire door, grabbed the crossbar, and shoved down. It didn't move. When he tried to pull it up, his hand slipped and he nearly fell on his back. The opposite door was the same—iron, sounding hollow when he kicked it, not budging when he put his shoulder to it and pushed as hard as he could. His soles slipped on the worn carpeting. His palms coated the bar with sweat and his fingers lost their grip.

No sweat, he thought; the other ones.

The other exits were locked.

Then he heard the scream.

The Orchard

Look for all these Tor books by Charles L. Grant

AFTER MIDNIGHT (Editor)
GREYSTONE BAY (Editor)
MIDNIGHT (Editor)
THE ORCHARD
NIGHTMARE SEASONS

DEDICATION

For Howard, who walks the land in the sun
        but never forgets midnight;
        who works in the city
        but comes home to Oxrun.
        My best man in many more ways than one.

Prologue

The Orchard

Charles L. Grant

TOR
HORROR

A TOM DOHERTY ASSOCIATES BOOK

THE ORCHARD

Copyright © 1986 by Charles L. Grant

First printing: December 1986

A TOR Book

Published by Tom Doherty Associates, Inc.
49 West 24 Street
New York, N.Y. 10010

Cover art by David Mann

ISBN: 0-812-51860-8
CAN. ED.: 0-812-51861-6

Printed in the United States of America

0 9 8 7 6 5 4 3 2 1

Old man Armstrong is dead, and no one since has claimed or worked the farm.

And whatever they were like, the man and his family, is a mystery best left to children's autumn dreams and the winter-long dreams of patient old men who lie awake until dawn, thinking of the time they wouldn't wake at all.

If there had ever been a farmhouse, substantial or not, it is gone—roof, walls, and foundation; if there had ever been a barn, a shed, outbuildings of any kind, they are gone as well, battered into the rocky soil or turned to wind-chased ash in the aftermath of a fire. No fence. No well. Not even a rutted road a wagon might have taken from the markets in the village. And the field that might once have been the site of high-growing corn, perhaps a green bed of alfalfa, perhaps lettuce rows or cabbage, is derelict now, and has been so for at least a century, if not more. Grasses whip-sharp and thin fill the furrows that are left, shrubs dream of being trees, and here and there for color an evergreen that has escaped being cut down for indoor use at Christmas. Dogs never run here, and cats seldom prowl, leaving the brown and green landscape to the insects and the crows.

To get there is easy: you cross Mainland Road, climb down and up a wide drainage ditch, then hunt for a decent gap in the wild thorned hedge that hides the land from the highway, and Oxrun Station beyond. Once through, and into the field, it remains a matter of not tripping over dead branches from trees you never saw, of avoiding the burrows that look to snare your ankles, of dodging the occasional hornet and slapping at gnats when the sun is near to setting.

Burrs cling to trousers, twigs snap under heels, and winter-raised rocks look to rob you of your balance.

Every so often, from somewhere just on the other side of my peripheral vision, I thought I saw a rabbit, stock-still, ears pricked, but turning showed me nothing but hillocks and tangled weeds. I even imagined a fox charging through the grass toward its den, pursued by a black hound—and that's when I decided that old man Armstrong, whoever he was, was right in leaving this place. It didn't hold dreams and it didn't hold nightmares, but in spite of the noise of the traffic behind me and the growl of an airliner stalking the blue above, it created images behind my eyes that I didn't want to see, didn't want to explore.

I shivered for no other reason than it felt right at the time, pushed my hands deep into the pockets of my worn denim jacket, and pushed on, using my knees to hack through those overgrown places I couldn't go around, telling myself for slim comfort this was the way the pioneers had done it, this was how it was when the village was born.

How nice for them, I thought glumly; no wonder they're all dead.

By the time I had gone a hundred yards, I felt as if I had been lifting weights all my life without benefit of pause, and I was damning those pioneers for coming here at all.

And what made it worse was the fact that Abe Stockton up there passed through it all as if he were a ghost.

"C'mon, Abe, give me a break, huh?"

He looked back and grinned at me, seeing my

puffing, my not too silent groaning, and pointed to the line of woodland north and south of the field. Dark walls. Hickory, pine, and oak. Birds sing there constantly that never sing here.

Then he nodded to the west, lifted the collar of his tan sheepskin coat, and ducked quickly away from a sudden violent gust that lifted dust from the dry ground and shoved it in our faces. When the air calmed and he had blinked his eyes clear, he inhaled slow and deep, and let it out in one explosion. A hand with a handkerchief wiped the sweat from his face. A hand covered his eyes, his mouth, and clenched into a fist.

I stopped feeling sorry for myself then and my less than perfect physical condition. At least I would be able to get out of bed tomorrow morning and go to work with the reasonable assumption that I'd do it all again the day after. And the day after that.

Abe Stockton couldn't.

Abe Stockton was dying.

"There," he said, pointing an old man's finger toward our destination. "Give it a couple of minutes more and you can rest, if you need it."

"Hell, I can walk all day if I have to," I lied with a grin. "Didn't I ever tell you about the time I managed eight thousand feet of Everest between breakfast and lunch?"

He smiled; he didn't laugh. I doubt anyone in

the Station has ever heard him really laugh, or has seen much more than that brief pull of his lips that narrows his face, squints his dark eyes, deepens the creases that mark him true New England. He is an unabashed and unashamed stereotype, no question about it, and he has been Chief of Police here for almost thirty-five years.

We ravaged a thicket with our boots and slashing arms, and once on the other side, he shook his head wearily and mopped his brow again.

"I ever tell you a Stockton was the first chief here, back a hundred years, maybe more? After the war, I think. Sonofabitch must have been ninety feet tall too, if you believe all the stories. I ever tell you about that?"

He had. He has, in fact, told me a lot of things over the two decades I've known him, much of which I've used in one form or another to chronicle the village's time, none of which he's told to anyone but me.

Which was why, now, we were going to the orchard.

"You gotta see it to believe it," he said to me yesterday afternoon, between prolonged bouts of coughing that turned his pale face red and tore his lungs apart. "Nothing I say is gonna make sense until you see it for yourself."

"But I have," I told him, thinking of the work I

hadn't done and had to get back to soon before the creditors decided to set up camp on my lawn. "I've been there a couple of times, as a matter of fact."

"Not with me, you haven't."

And that sealed it; I was going.

A hundred yards later we were there, seated on a rock large enough to hold ten, dark enough to trap midnight and never give back the stars.

The orchard must have been a wonderful place, back when it was alive and no one stayed away— scores of twisted apple trees whose fruit scented the air each fall and turned the land red once the first frost had passed; the blossoms in spring must have looked like snow from a distance, an entire field of it daring the sun to melt it down; the sound of children picking their own for pies and pre-serves and butter and cakes must have brought Christmas early to this part of the world.

It must have been great.

It's more than dismal now.

Most of the original trees are long gone, and of those that remain, only a handful have been un-touched by an unexplained fire that raged here nearly ten years ago. Trunks and branches are charred; the grass in most places has never re-turned; rain has pounded the ash into a crust on the ground. If any fruit still matures on the plants that

14

can still bear them, they probably drop unnoticed to the dead ground, and probably rot.

"Ugly little place, isn't it," he said, taking the handkerchief out again to wipe his face and neck dry.

I nodded; but it isn't, not really, though it is without question unpleasant—the images that had stalked me across the field darkened here and grew shadows, shifted contrary to the wind and played darkly around the boles, and I wished we could have stayed back at his house while he told me what he had to. At least there I would be out of the damp cold and in a comfortable chair, with a drink in my left hand and his old bloodhound snoring in volleys at my right; at least there I could turn a lamp on after sunset, listen to the radio, watch a little TV, read his newspaper while he fussed with dinner in the kitchen.

At least there I wouldn't have to see the shadows of the dead.

A spasm of coughing and choking bent him over, and I could do nothing but pat his shoulder helplessly until it was done, angry that he was going to leave me at last, angry that I couldn't do anything to make the leaving easy, angry that no doctor could tell him what the hell was wrong.

"Yep," he said, his breath back and his grin. "First chief in town was old Lucas. They had the police before, of course, but he was the first one dumb enough to take the job.''

"He wasn't exactly dumb," I said, shivering. "He did all right, from what you've told me."

"Did all right with what he had, I suppose." He squinted at the light, shook out the handkerchief, and blew his nose. "His son became chief too, y'know. Ned, it was. They never called him anything else. Some say I tend to favor him more than my own father." He wiped his mouth; his hand was trembling.

"Abe, look," I said, "why don't we go back, okay? There's—"

"I never planned on living this long, y'know," he said, ignoring me as always and staring at the trees as if they were about to uproot themselves and come at him. "Never planned it, never wanted it, if you want to know the truth. I was gonna die peacefully at eighty in my bed, an ornery old coot who didn't give a damn about much of anything but making his peace with the Lord." He gripped his knees and lowered his head, but not his eyes. "But things just got outta hand, son. I never had a say, and they just got outta hand." He sniffed, and spat. "Too much to take care of, pups to train to be cops in the Station, city folks to watch out for in case they broke a leg crossing the street. Every goddamn time I took a vacation they put that idiot

Windsor in, took me weeks to clean up after him. Shame he's dead, I guess, but he was a jackass.'' His gaze lowered, to the ground. ''It ain't been easy, y'know. Jesus God, it ain't been easy.''

I didn't have to answer; I knew what he meant.

It wasn't the small amount of crime we have here in Oxrun, or the people he had to teach, or the sicknesses he endured all alone in his home.

It was the other things.

The far side of the shadow things that no one ever believes until they wake up past midnight, cold and unsettled, and see the landscape of the night-world that exists beyond the far boundaries of legend, beyond the frail cage of reason; the dark children of their childhoods who have gleefully persisted through education, through marriages, through living in the modern world, and wait under the stairs to laugh quietly and harsh; the shade of black seen only when eyes are open and dawn hasn't arrived and a wind shakes the doorknob like the paw of a wolf learning to come in; the light that dances without fire and glows without a bulb and casts no shadow in the corner of the room where something small and large crouches behind the chair.

The other things.

He reached into his coat then and pulled out a manila folder creased in half and filled with papers.

"It's not a will," he said, his smile one-sided. "These are for you. From my office. I don't think anybody else would bother to check them."

"Abe, don't you think—"

He waved me silent and stood, one hand back to the boulder to balance himself. "Back in a minute. Have a look, in the meantime, and let me know what you think."

Then he did the oddest thing—he reached out and shook my hand.

The sun was shining.

It was early November.

There was no reason in the world why I should have felt the way I did, but when I looked at the first page, read the names, saw the places, it was winter already, deep in a January whose air was ancient parchment and whose moon gave no light.

It was always winter when Abe showed me these things, and I glanced up at him, wondering how he had managed to carry it all without going mad, without climbing to the attic and locking himself in and waiting . . . waiting for the dark landscape to come and take him home.

So he walked, and I read, and when I looked up again I could see the first stars and the first arc of the new moon.

THE ORCHARD

I could see the orchard the way it was, and the way it was now.

And I buttoned my jacket, folded the papers and held them, and thought about the good dreams I never had as a child.

Part One

My Mary's Asleep

I don't care for the dark when there isn't any light, when there's not even a hint of something else out there, when I feel that a single step will drop me over the edge, when my ears hear nothing but the blood (god, the blood) and my hands feel nothing but the cold (oh god, the cold) and my eyes see nothing but the fire and the sparks and the whorls of a scream that crouches deep in my throat;

I don't care for the dark when there isn't any glow, not in the sky, not in the village, not under the trees where I'm waiting, a glow that's a sign there are people out there who aren't much different than I, who would understand what I know, who would hold me while I tell them, who would protect me from the others and tell them they're wrong;

And I don't care for the dark when my Mary's not here.

Twilight, that last night we were all together, was a flawless study in lovers' pastels—a deep and soothing rose around the edges of snowlike dark clouds, bright pink flaring from the rim of the sun resting below the horizon, robin's-egg blue and gentle turquoise splashing over and blending with a faint and fading gold floating ahead of a faint and fading black. It softened the serrations on the oak leaves overhead, smoothed out the bark until the shadows were gone, and nestled in cotton a mockingbird's song.

A twilight so perfect it seemed sacrilege to take even a single breath, or even let my heart beat on the last night, that night, when I started to die.

Yet it was, to my mind, incredibly like a number of paintings good and bad I had seen, and as I stared at the sky I wondered why artists bothered to put any of it to music, or to canvas, or on a printed page. Didn't they know, couldn't they see, that their work would suffer when compared with the real thing?

Unless this was what they felt just before they

cast their slim and ruined bodies over the cliff, into the sea.

"Oh, Jesus, Herb, come *on*," I muttered in disgust, and my nose wrinkled with embarrassment at the lurid image of the grieving poet, giving all for love—that was the fool's way out. Only a fool pines, only a fool sighs. Only a fool gives his life for someone who doesn't care.

So fool, I thought, what do you do now?

My cheeks were cupped in my hands, my elbows braced on the soft ground, the toes of my sneakers idly digging trenches behind me. The air was spring sweet, and I closed my eyes to smell it, taste it, moisten my lips as if I had just finished a succulent meal; the late afternoon was lightly chilled, but I didn't reach for my jacket lying on the grass at my side. Instead, I rolled onto my back and stared at the branches, wishing on their curves that Mary was here.

Alone. With me.

"Fat chance, jerk," I muttered, and winced at the choice of words.

I had resolved only moments before that nothing resembling the word or the fact of fat would pass my lips again until I had lost fifty pounds from the over two hundred I already weighed. And once fifty was gone, maybe twenty more in the bargain. In the meantime, I would work to reconstruct my self-image, build up my confidence, and see my-self differently when I looked in the mirror. Fat was out, then, and overweight was in. Hell, lots of people were overweight without looking like a washtub with spokes for arms and legs; lots of people went on diets just to maintain their health, for crying out loud. So it would have to be with me. Not fat. Certainly not obese. Just looking after myself so I would live past forty.

"Fat chance," I said again, this time with a grin. I knew myself too well, though I was hoping this time I would wake up to a surprise.

I sat up with a grunt, then, fished for my jacket, and slipped it on before standing. I supposed I should be doing something constructive before the others arrived, like spreading the blankets I'd brought, or checking the woods and open fields to be sure we wouldn't be attacked by tigers or lost lions. Or maybe, I thought, I should just forget the whole thing and go home—not later, but right now, before I could think of some new way to stall. There was still work to be done on my final project, and I wasn't exactly sure how I would present it.

Then someone called my name, and I surren-dered to fate.

* * *

I don't remember whose idea it first was, but after enduring nearly a full month of final-exam threats from cackling professors and sadistic young instructors who knew all the right words to set terror on our heels, it didn't matter. We had to get away. It was Friday, and we had to try to pretend we really didn't give a damn, that it was all going to be a snap and graduation with honors was only a matter of killing the next year without getting arrested.

We decided to have our picnic on the deserted Armstrong farm, in the shade of the orchard that didn't grow anything anymore.

What the hell—we were in college and didn't know any better.

So Stick Reese brought the wine, Mike Buller the sandwiches, and the others—there were about a dozen—brought the odds and ends, including a case of cold beer. The plans as we had so cleverly figured it would be to enjoy ourselves while studying for the legalized torture that would begin bright and early Monday morning. The collected condemneds' last meal, and who gave a shit.

But the not unexpected result was the packing away of the books as soon as they were brought out, and a prolonged bitch session about our classes, the college, and the world that conspired to prevent us from getting rich. There was also a baseball game with acorns, and a scientific experiment to see how far one could shove an arm down a burrow before the gopher got pissed and chewed the thing off.

Mary had come with Rich Verner, and she spent most of her time sitting under a tree and whispering in his ear.

I, the stoic and unheralded lover, sat against my own apple tree on the orchard's rim and dispensed facile wisdom while keeping an eye on the round of her shoulder, the curve of her breast, the way her legs in their jeans seemed never to stop.

Only Reese knew I was lovesick and thankfully kept his cracks to a minimum; we had known each other since high school, and he had seen me moping and glooming around like this before, and for some damn reason had decided some time ago it was his duty to keep me from slashing my wrists or hanging myself or doing something really stupid, like proposing to the girl.

"Y'know," he said, after we had eaten and the others had drifted off, "what you ought to do, pal, is walk right over there, punch Rich out, and drag Mary into the bushes."

"Sounds good," I said, and clamped my teeth hard on a ham sandwich.

"Hey, I'm not shitting you, man," he insisted, and squirmed around so he was sitting in front of me, his backwards baseball cap crammed down harder, his right hand—the one without the beer can—flicking at his chin. He was trying to grow a beard; he wasn't doing very well. "Really. The caveman stuff, y'know?"

I swallowed and gave him the eye. "Just leave it, all right?"

He looked at me, testing, then showed me a set of teeth that better belonged on a dumb horse. "Take it from me," he said. "They like that macho crap. All this stuff about sensitivity and caring and garbage like that—hell, if it was true, she'd be all over you in a minute."

There was a compliment in there somewhere, and when I found it, I thanked him, though it didn't do me a bit of good.

"Don't mention it, Herb. No sweat." He rocked back and spread his hands behind him. "You see, your problem is—"

"Who's got a problem?" another voice asked.

Wonderful, I thought; bring on the United Nations while you're at it.

Stick looked up at Mike Buller and nodded toward me. Mike, in turn, looked to the sky and shook his head wearily, as if to tell whoever was watching to look out, the fat boy was at it again with all his whining about unrequited love. A loud and heavy sigh, a drooping of his head, and he

29

looked up at me and winked. He was carrying an overloaded tray of food he'd gotten from his father's market over on Steuben Avenue, the one that used to be Garland's until old man Garland ran off with a produce clerk and his wife sold the place and moved down to Georgia. Without dropping a single sandwich, he handed it to Amy Niles and sat down. Amy stuck out her tongue, blew a kiss to me, and walked off to serve the animals their second course.

Mary was still under the tree with Verner.

"Don't tell me," Mike said, put his fingertips dramatically to his temples, and closed his eyes. He claimed to want to be a stage magician when he grew up, which meant, to me, he would probably end up working behind his father's counter for the rest of his life. "I see . . . yes, I see a redhead."

"Knock it off, Mike," I said.

As usual, he ignored me.

"I see a redhead with hair down to her ass, legs up to her neck, and a smile that keeps Professor Danvers sitting behind his desk whenever she asks a question." His eyes opened. "Am I right, or am I right?"

"A real pal," I told him.

Stick laughed with a palm over his mouth.

"Look," I said, "it isn't funny anymore, okay? I'm asking you nice just to knock it off."

Stick laughed again.

Mike slapped his shoulder, hard, and began pluck-ing the grass. "It's a bitch. Christ, it's a pain." He was serious. He knew what I was going through because he was going through it with Amy. And frankly, I was getting a little tired of holding his sweaty hand.

For a while, shortly after Mary Oster really and truly came into my life at the start of this semester, I had hopes she would see through the weight I was carrying and maybe, just maybe, like what was in there. My uncle, when I thought it was the right time to confide in him, told me straight out I was a jerk, that as long as I kept stuffing my face with everything in the kitchen there wasn't a woman on the planet who would give me a second glance; my aunt May told me the same thing, but in a way that didn't make me feel like so much shit.

"You have to make up your mind, Herb," she said. "You have to know what you want, and what you think is important. Life isn't like the movies. Miracles don't happen on their own."

I didn't like her very much for a while after that, even though I knew she was right. And for the first time in I don't know when, I found myself wishing my mother hadn't died and my father hadn't taken off to god knows where. The Alstars may be family, and the only family I had, but it was obvious to me then that they just didn't understand.

So I consoled my miseries with the memory of a film I had seen on campus the month before—*Beauty and the Beast*, a lyrical French adaptation that haunted me for days . . . until I decided that fairy tales, for me, were only another form of self-pity. I was fat, not a beast, and flame-haired Mary wasn't about to be my Beauty, my Esmeralda, or even the princess who could change frogs to princes.

A breeze began to blow, and Stick wondered if there'd be rain.

No Beast, but something worse.

Toni Keane, who was popping grapes under a nearby tree, demanded to know who'd brought the umbrellas.

No enemy, but something worse.

I was Mary's friend, a good friend, and never destined to be more.

Christ, now that *is* a bitch. Liberated philosophies aside, being a close friend of a woman you're in love with is a torture I wouldn't even wish on my stupid uncle, even if he is a judge.

I must have made some kind of noise, because Stick looked at me kind of funny, but before he could ask me what I was thinking—I could see the damned question just waiting there on his lips—

Amy returned with the empty tray and sat down, close to Mike but not close enough. He and I exchanged glances of the damned, and he started to whistle.

I felt a chill. I looked to the sky. When I couldn't find a decent cloud, I looked behind me, into that part of the orchard that had been burned black and stayed that way.

Then Toni roused herself long enough to crawl over, give us all a disgusted look, and demand, "So when does the orgy start, huh?"

Amy blushed a little, but she was still a freshman and we managed to forgive her.

"Well?" Toni said, rising up on her knees, her hands on her hips and her t-shirt pulling snug across her small breasts. "God, are you guys dead or something?"

Suddenly, I started to laugh. It was, on the face and every other part of it, ludicrous. So goddamned ludicrous. Most of us were juniors in college, practically grown up and ready to assault the world, and we were behaving like we were dumbass horny freshmen in search of the perfect lay.

It was infectious.

Stick laughed.

Amy laughed.

Mike did his best to keep a straight face, but

one look at Toni, who was sticking her tongue out at him, and he blew up so loudly a flock of crows took to the air.

We rolled, we giggled, we did everything but fall into each other's arms. It was a while before we calmed down, and by then the others had wandered up, looking for something to do now that the food was gone. Before I knew it, they were gathered around me like disciples in front of a blond and blue-eyed Buddha. For a moment, a frightening moment, I thought Stick would say something, or that they'd start in on me, teasing me, offering me advice about the latest fad diets. But Amy, for which I vowed to love her forever, said something about my uncle Gil and the way he had come down hard on some friends of hers in court because of a party the week before, and the bust that followed. No one was jailed, but the people who had complained about the noise and the drinking had insisted the offenders do public service as penance. My uncle agreed.

"The park," Amy said, "won't have a shred of litter in it from now until the Second Coming, for god's sake."

She wanted to know then if I had influence with him, but I couldn't answer because Toni demanded that I appeal to his better nature and well-known love for students and ask him to close down the campus because conditions there were horrifyingly inhumane.

"What do you mean, inhumane?" Stick asked, as always about ten minutes behind the rest of the world.

Amy gave him an example. Mike gave him another. Even Richard yelled something over, and within minutes there was practically a committee set to start the revolution. It didn't take long to draw up a list of grievances each more outrageous than the last; and when the laughter was over, Amy leapt to her feet, snatched off Stick's cap and started running.

He yelled and chased her.

Rich dove for her and missed.

Someone else yelled at Stick, and the next thing I knew we were involved in a game that had no rules, had no goals—we got up and we ran, eventually working ourselves into a wild session of tag with no home base and no object other than to let off the steam the bitching didn't vent.

Even I did it.

By definition and point of bulk, I'm not the fastest guy in the known universe. For as long as I could remember, my size has always provoked comments, and I finally decided I wasn't ever going to play the role of jolly fat man, fat clown, stumbling, bumbling, uncoordinated jackass. I fought back, and did so all my life, and won enough times to let all but the dumbest of strangers know that fat jokes and snide remarks need not apply when it came to needling Herbert Johns.

I think . . . I *think* that's why I had true friends instead of those who kept me around just for laughs.

So I was fairly able to hold my own once the chase got out of the field and into the trees. Diabolical shrubs held no terror for me, ambushing branches quailed at my passing, and I managed, once, to get a good hard hand on Rich's shoulder, hard enough to send him pinwheeling into a thornbush whose greeting had him bellowing for revenge.

I laughed and charged on.

The light faded as we played, and eventually I followed Mary when we all returned to the orchard, Stick and Amy right behind me, Mike and Rich bringing up the rear. Toni hadn't even gotten to her feet. She just sat there, grinning like an idiot and finishing my lunch.

It was chilly in there, almost nightcold under the fire-blackened trees, and the footing was less stable than out in the field. Several times I thought I was going to fall; a couple of times more I thought I could see someone else with us, someone not a kid. But my heart was pounding and my focus not exactly clear, and we finally made it into the open without anyone breaking a leg. The only casualty was me—a scrape along my forehead when I didn't duck fast enough.

Mary, by that time, was laughing so hard she could barely move, but she kept ahead of me, and once we broke out into the open again, she headed for the blankets and safety, while the others swung wide to the east, aiming for Mainland Road. I didn't have a prayer of catching her, and I knew it; but god, it was nice, and there was always that hope that Rich wouldn't suddenly pop out and call her, put his arm around her waist, and prove to us how he owned her by giving her a light scolding and a long kiss.

He didn't.

Mary fell.

And I fell beside her.

"Jesus, Herb," she said as she rolled out of my way. "Are you trying to crush me to death?"

"Only in the mad throes of my unbridled passion," I panted, rolling the other way and sitting up, hands on my thighs, my heart telling me I ought to know better than lug my fat around like that.

She giggled, coughed, pushed her hair out of her eyes, and pulled a handkerchief from her jeans pocket. With an appraising look that made me feel like a slightly soiled side of pork, she knelt in front of me and began mopping the sweat from my face, the dirt from around my cut.

"Uh, Mary . . ."

"Shut up, Herb. I'm playing nurse."

Without moving my head, I glanced around, looking for Rich. He was still involved with Stick and the rest, and I think I saw Mike deliberately leading him farther away. Toni had left; I never knew where she went.

When I looked back, Mary was staring at me, her head tilted to one side. "Not bad," she said.

"I do my best."

She sat on her heels and pulled her long hair over one shoulder, stroking it absently as she looked up at the sky over the orchard, at the colors that still clung there stubbornly, ahead of the dark. "Pretty."

"Like Hollywood."

"Better. It's real."

I agreed, and couldn't think of anything else to say until, in a flash of brilliance that has been my problem for years, I asked what she was doing for her year-end project.

"A self-portrait," she said, and blushed. "You think that's silly?"

I didn't think so, not for her.

What was silly was that I had been taking art courses since my freshman year, conned into the first one by Stick, who had sworn to me on his dead moped's grave that it would be so easy I could walk through it in my sleep. Incredibly, he was right. Too right, as a matter of fact, because with the help of my teachers I uncovered a certain amount of reasonable talent I didn't know I had. Nothing spectacular. I wasn't going to be the overaged Mozart of the art world or anything. But I was good enough to be truly encouraged, and I improved enough over the next couple of years so that I was beginning to believe I might actually make a living at it in some small way—a commercial artist, maybe, or something like that.

This year, though, I discovered—from, of all people, my stupid uncle—that whittling was actually a form of sculpture most people ignored because they thought it was only a bunch of old men sitting in old chairs turning sticks into shavings. Before I knew it, I was learning about the best kinds of wood to use, the right kinds of blades for this style and that . . . and it fascinated me. The trouble was, with oils and acrylics I was comfortable; with the other stuff, though, from stone to wood to collages made from old magazines and old clothes, my projects seemed more like the results of insane demolition.

So naturally, good old Professor Danvers tells us we were supposed to do our year-end final in whatever medium we were worst at. *Pick a subject,* he told us; *animal or human, and do something unusual with it. It doesn't have to be great. I just want to see what you've learned about technique. And if you've overcome your handicaps, as it were, and have conquered the enemy.*

He thought it was funny.

I saw my average falling to its death from the top of the chapel.

Then, in probably what will be the only true inspiration I'll ever have in my life, I got an idea when I saw a special on Westminster Abbey. If I pulled it off, I'd be a genius; if I didn't, maybe the old bastard would take pity and not fail me too badly.

"Damnit, Herb!" Mary said then, seeing the vacant look on my face and knowing I wasn't listening.

"Sorry," I said sheepishly.

"C'mon, do you think it's silly or not?"

"What?"

She looked at the ground as if searching for something to throw at me. "The self-portrait! Do you think it's silly?"

Mary, as much as I loved her, was definitely not an artist.

"No, it's not silly. But . . ."

"It's not unusual, I know." She pushed her hair

back and sighed. "I think I'm going to do it in something like glass or scraps of paper." Her grin was sly. "He'll think I'm avant-garde or something."

"You believe that?"

She tried to look serious, failed and laughed. "Not for a minute, but I'm no artist, for Christ's sake. Not like you are. It's all Stick's fault anyway. He swore to me it would be a gut course, y'know? I could walk through it in my sleep."

I must have gaped, because she started giggling and could barely ask what was wrong with me. When I told her Reese had given me the same sales pitch, she was ready to get up and murder him and the hell with the death penalty. I suggested it would ruin her college career. She suggested I shove it.

"What about you, Herb? What are you doing?"

The gold was gone, the rose and the pink. There was nothing left but a hint of the sun.

"Wood," I told her reluctantly. "Something in wood."

"Really? Some kind of sculpture?"

"Sort of."

She pouted. "You won't tell me, will you."

"I can't, Mary. I . . . can't."

Her disappointment was strong enough to cloud her eyes, and I couldn't help wondering why she was here, sitting with me instead of running off with darling Richard. I shifted uneasily, the damp ground beginning to work its way through my jeans.

A crow called, and she followed its coasting flight over the trees. Behind her I could see the dimming branches of the orchard, and I shivered when I thought of the run through it. No one went in there. Not even in fun. I don't know why, but I thought then it was probably because it was so gloomy.

"You're losing weight, huh?"

I had to blink and force my attention back. "What?"

Her hand fluttered through the space in front of my chest before landing on my left arm. "I said, it looks like you're losing a little weight. You on a diet?"

I almost hit her. Flattery is okay, but not when it's so obvious, and so obviously wrong. I shook my head, though, and slapped my hands against my stomach. "I wish I were. As a matter of fact, I'm going to, real soon now."

She kept on looking at me, frowning so hard I couldn't help but look down at myself. And when I did, I grunted my surprise. Either my clothes had stretched themselves to their limit in anticipation of the next two weeks' worth of meals, or I really was, honest to god, losing a few pounds.

"Son of a bitch."

"See?" she said brightly. Green eyes wide now, and laughing; green eyes I wanted to jump into and live in; green eyes that darkened when she saw how I watched them.

"Don't," she said quietly. "Don't even think it."

And I was saved from lying by the sound of a horn, the sound of a scream, the sound of a car braking too late.

Mainland Road is only two lanes wide, and the only way past the Station. On the east side is a tight wall of evergreens, which prevents drivers from seeing the village unless they turn directly into one of the streets; on the west there's a wide, graveled shoulder, a shallow ditch, and a climb through thick hedges and brush before you reach the Armstrong farm.

There's not much traffic, even at this time of day.

But he was lying in the ditch anyway, a pants leg torn from knee to ankle, one shoe half off, and from the angle of his head and the blood bubbling at his lips, I knew he was dead.

Mary screamed and jumped down to cradle him in her arms.

While Stick, ghost-pale himself, tried to pull her away, Mike took off up the highway, trying to catch the license plate of the car that didn't stop; someone else, maybe it was Toni, had the presence of mind to run up Chancellor Avenue, heading for the police.

It wasn't me.

I stood at the top of the rise and kept telling myself how wrong, how evil, how goddamned *sick* it was that I should feel glad Rich Verner was dead.

I almost threw up.

But I couldn't turn away, not even when Mary looked up at me and pleaded.

I know I didn't move when a patrol car came screaming across the road, and right behind it an ambulance; I know I didn't say a word when Mike came back, puffing, stumbling, admitting his failure in a loud string of obscenities that had Amy weeping.

It was full dark now.

My perfect twilight had ended.

Instead, red and blue spinning lights turned everything a strobic and sickly purple; people walked through stabbing flashlight and spotlight like disjointed black ghosts. Voices whispered, asked questions, gave orders, faded away.

The streetlamps came on and made the night darker.

And when Stick finally came to stand beside me after the police and ambulance had gone, I tried hard to make him think I was miserable; I didn't have to pretend I was cold.

"We might as well go home, Herb, huh?"

I shrugged.

He kicked at a rock and sent it skittering into the road. "Mary went with him to the hospital."

There was a faint, annoying buzzing in my ears, almost like whispering.

He turned his cap around and slipped his hands into his belt, thumbs out and drumming. "You suppose the cops'd mind if we waited until tomorrow to clean up the mess back there?"

I shrugged again, and rubbed a finger along my ear to drive the sound away.

"C'mon, pal," he said softly. "They'll catch the bastard, don't worry. We gotta go. C'mon, we gotta go. There's nothing left to do."

I let him push me a bit with his hip, let him start down the slope to the ditch before I followed, clumsily, my head feeling as if it had been pumped full of winter air, my arms and legs so suddenly weightless I had the horrible sensation that I was actually flying. It made the food in my stomach turn to acid; it made my vision blur so that I had to stretch out a hand to keep myself from falling.

"Herb?"

"Yeah?"

"You okay? You want some help?"

Stick. Good old Stick. Labeled that way since kindergarten because he looked like a skeleton someone had dressed in used clothes. Taking hold of my arm like I was an old man or something and leading me up the avenue, saying nothing, whistling without a tune, pulling me across the street when we reached the police station because there was a man in a dark suit standing on the steps, watching us. It was Detective Gilman, and he turned his head as we passed, probably not letting us go until we disappeared around the corner of Raglin and didn't come back.

Good old Stick. Always there when you need him, and even when you don't. Opening the gate and guiding me up the walk, ringing the doorbell and explaining to Aunt May what had happened, that I was all right, just a little funny because Rich was my friend.

She thanked him and gathered me in, called out to Uncle Gil, and took me up the stairs.

Put me to bed.

And did not say a word about the noise that was

so loud, so persistent, I was positive she could hear.

The noise no longer like whispering, but like a dry cold wind sifting through dead leaves.

Richard was dead, and I was glad, and Mary had seen it all in my eyes.

I stayed in bed most of Saturday morning. I didn't dream the night before—I don't remember dreaming, at least—but I slept badly, wrestling with the blanket, punching the pillow, several times coming up hard against the wall as I rolled around in search of someplace to give me peace.

When I did waken at last, May was sitting at my desk, watching me anxiously. She was young, my mother's baby sister, and not very much older than I. A slender, blonde woman who seemed, when I was having fantasies of great power, to be more my type than the type she had married.

"How are you feeling?"

I almost sat up, then realized my clothes were gone and there were no pajamas in their place. I think I blushed; I know she grinned.

"Okay, I guess." I waited for the buzzing. When I didn't hear it, I smiled. "Okay."

"Gil wants to talk to you, if you feel up to it."

I groaned and fell back on the pillow. "Do I have to?"

47

"No, of course not. But he's worried. He . . . he remembers."

I knew without her telling me. I knew that, until last night, the only other time I had seen a person dead was when I found my mother in her kitchen, lying all twisted around on the floor under the table my father had made one Easter. When I told my father, he beat me for not keeping an eye on her. I was only five, but I was supposed to watch her when I was home because she had a bad heart. The heart stopped. My father stopped beating me when my arms began to bleed. Then he arranged for the funeral, the burial plot, and for his sister-in-law to look after me while, as he put it, he hunted for new employment in some other place besides this miserable hole.

He never came back.

The dreams did, forever.

"I'm okay," I told her again. "Really. I don't want to talk."

She waited to see if I was telling the truth, then nodded and came over to the bed. I could smell lemon oil on her hands as she tucked the sheet around my neck and ordered me, smiling, to stay where I was until she brought something up to fill my tank.

"I'm not hungry."

"I can see that. I think you even look a bit

thinner. But you have to eat something, boy, to keep your strength up." She kissed the tip of her finger and placed the finger on my forehead, a comfort when I was little, a little disturbing now. "You still have those exams, Herb. You don't want to get sick."

"Exams?"

God, didn't she realize what had happened last night? Didn't she know?

"Yes, exams," she said sternly. "This is a bad time for something like this to happen, I can understand that. But you can't let it throw you, you hear? You've got to be strong, Herb. You've got to be strong. For yourself, as well as your friends."

"That's an understatement," I muttered sourly.

She left without saying anything else, and I closed my eyes, saw Rich bleeding in the ditch, and opened them again. This is dumb, I thought; this is really dumb. He wasn't anything near as bad as my mother, but I just couldn't shake him.

Dumb.

Really dumb.

Finally, when my back and buttocks ached so much I couldn't lie down anymore, I got up, dressed, sat at the desk, and tried to do a little studying. After an hour I could barely keep my head from falling off my shoulders, so I lay down again and promptly fell asleep.

There were no dreams, or none that I could remember.

But when I awakened for the second time that day, the sun was down and there was the smell of food cooking deliciously in the kitchen. My stomach made like a geyser ready to blow, and I jumped off the bed, ran down the stairs, and only barely restrained myself from charging into the dining room.

No one was there.

I walked around the table and into the kitchen.

It was empty.

The oven was off, there were no pots or pans on the stove, nothing waiting on the table. I was a little confused and scratched the sleep from my eyes, squinted, and saw a note on the counter from my aunt, telling me she and Uncle Gil had gone to the movies in the new theater in town, and that I'd had a couple of phone calls while I was napping. She said she didn't want to wake me up because she knew what I was going through.

Stick had been in touch, and Mike, and Mary (she underlined the name) three times.

Rubbing a nervous hand over my stomach to calm it down, I hurried into the living room and sat in my uncle's chair, pulled the telephone into my lap, and dialed Stick's number first—he and Mike would be the quickest to get through, and by then I would have worked up enough nerve to concentrate on Mary.

It took a while to get to talk to Reese, though. First I got his father, who was, by the sound of it, halfway through his ninth case of beer. He wasn't all that bad a guy, not really, but he'd been out of work for over two years, laid off by the railroad and unable to get anything else but the occasional odd job. I let him jabber, made the right sounds Uncle Gil had taught me, then asked again for Stick.

I heard some muffled yelling, and what could have been a slap. Then: "Hey, man, how you doing?"

Good old Stick.

I told him I wasn't too bad, all things considered, and asked if the cops had found the hit-and-run driver yet.

"No way. That guy was a hundred years gone before we even got there, remember?"

"Damn. I thought Mike saw him, the car anyway. Did anyone else see it?"

I heard someone popping bubble gum like a machine gun then, heard Stick yell at his kid sister to get the hell out of the room, right now, god-damnit, and preferably not stopping until she reached Alaska.

"Nothing," he said when he came back. "I don't know. It's like . . . Shit, I don't know."

I straightened a little; he didn't sound quite right. "Hey, you okay?"

"Oh, yeah," he said. "I've just been thinking, y'know? Rich was my age. My age, you know what I mean?"

"Right. I . . . right." I wish he hadn't reminded me. His age was my age, and I sure didn't want to talk about mortality just now.

We yakked a bit more, about the exams, about how rotten things were, then he asked me about the stupid game we had played.

I looked at my watch. "What about it?"

"You went through the orchard, right?"

"Well, sure! Only a zillion yards ahead of you, that's all."

His laugh was short and dry. "When you went through, Herb, or when we were sitting there, did you . . . this is dumb, but did you kind of feel something?"

"What?" Jesus, I thought; Rich's dying really got to him, bad. "I don't know what you're talking about, man."

"The cold, Herb. Didn't you feel the cold?"

I thought, and I remembered. "Yeah, sure. What about it?"

"Weird, huh?"

"No, it wasn't weird, for god's sake. It was almost dark. And it ain't the middle of July, in case you hadn't noticed. What did you want, ninety degrees or something?"

"Oh, absolutely," he said, too loud and too fast. "I am a Sunbelt baby, remember? Born and practically bred in the wilds of Miami, and I don't intend to spend the rest of my stupid life in this stupid icebox." He yelled at his sister again and apologized, saying he was stuck at home, babysitting, because his father wasn't feeling well and his mom was out at some meeting at their church.

"No sweat," I told him and we agreed to meet at the student union after the English exam; tomorrow being Sunday, he had to stay home, help his mom around the house and do the yard work. I knew he wanted to bitch some about it, but I didn't give him the chance. I told him Mike had called, and I promised to get back to him if there was any gossip he should know.

"Good deal," he said. "Maybe he knows who that joker was who crashed the picnic."

"Joker? What joker? Stick, who are you—"

Then his little sister screamed bloody murder right in my ear and the line went dead, and I knew if I called back, I'd get his father again.

Mike wasn't home. His mother said he had gone over to Amy's just a little while ago and—she laughed—he wasn't in the best of moods. She called it a lovers' spat; I watched my language and told her she was probably right.

Then I took a deep breath, said a few prayers to anyone who was listening, and dialed Mary's number.

She answered on the third ring, and she sounded like hell.

"The funeral's Monday afternoon," she said.

I leaned back and stared at the ceiling, feeling like a shit for not feeling a thing. "You want company?"

"I don't know if I can go." Then she started crying, the dry kind that makes you want to scratch your throat because suddenly it feels like it's been filled with sand. "I don't know, Herb, I don't know. What should I do?"

"He was our friend," I told her as gently and truthfully as I could. "He was a buddy. We should."

"He wanted me to marry him!"

Oh, hell, I thought.

"He said we could wait until after graduation and then get married." The crying stopped; she had the hiccoughs now. "He said we could have our own careers, you know? He said we didn't have to have children until later."

I didn't want to hear it. I didn't want to know it.

But I couldn't stop her because she didn't know me. So I sat there for nearly an hour while she told me all the plans she and Rich had made, and how her life was ruined because some asshole in some asshole car was too damned drunk to see where he was going.

"Mary," I said at last, "calm down, huh? Take it easy."

"It just isn't fair that he's dead! Damnit, Herb, it just isn't fair!"

I didn't say anything. I let her go on until, finally, she dropped into a silence that had me thinking, after a minute, that she'd hung up.

Then, softly: "I'm sorry, Herb. I didn't mean—"

"It's all right, okay? It's all right."

"Are you angry?"

"With you? C'mon, Mary, don't be a jerk. Unless you want me to be."

"What?"

"I mean, if you really want me to be mad at you, I will."

"Herb, please . . ."

"No, I mean it sincerely. Of course, you realize I'll have to come over there and hang you from the ceiling by your thumbs and give you forty lashes with a wet cat."

She giggled.

"You want me to come over? I can pick up a cat on the way."

"No," she said, reluctantly. "I can't see anyone, I don't think. I look like hell and I can't stop crying and Jesus Christ, why the fuck did it have to happen to him?"

I had no answers, but I think I did a fair job of telling her so in the right way because the hiccoughs soon stopped and she was sort of laughing again.

"Jesus, Herb, what would I do without you?"

"Stagger on somehow," I told her in my best, lousy British accent. "Chins up, eyes forward, pulling yourself together with a paper clip and a hammer."

Another laugh, a quiet thanks, and we rang off.

I sat there forever, staring at the receiver, squinting at the far wall, finally pushing myself to my feet and heading for the back door. I needed to think. I needed to tell myself that it just wasn't done, what I was thinking, which was to make myself so available to handle her grief that Mary would never think of being without me again.

In the old days, they called jerks like that cads.

I paused in the kitchen, sniffing the air vainly for the cooking smells I had noticed before, and shrugged. It must have been a reaction to the fact I hadn't eaten all day, and my diet-killing mind was bringing up fond memories of Aunt May's best meals. But since I still wasn't all that hungry, I continued on outside, into a backyard walled in by house-high pines, the grass perfectly mowed, the flowers under the windows all the same height. My uncle's doing. And the only break in the symmetry he had forced on it was a small shed in the back. Green, and the one place I could go and not be disturbed.

It used to be Uncle Gil's toolshed until he got tired of doing all the work himself and hired a gardener; now it was my studio, heated for winter, a couple of small windows to keep me from frying in summer. After a glance back at the house, I unlocked the door behind me, and switched on the light.

And I hadn't taken two steps toward the workbench and my project beside it when someone started pounding on the walls.

"It's Amy, that goddamned little bitch!" Mike yelled as he bulled in when I reopened the door.

At first I thought she must be dead or in a coma, but the way he ranted around the room, the way he looked for something to throw and didn't even dare pick up a pencil, told me she had zapped his ego again.

"You know what she said?" His face was flushed

the color of roses, and he couldn't stop waving his arms. "Do you have any idea what she just said to me?"

I didn't, and I dragged him quickly outside before he destroyed everything I had. Immediately, he flopped onto the grass and began pulling it out by the roots.

"What," I said, not getting down beside him. "What's going on now?"

"She said . . . god, I still can't believe it. She said that she's decided she can't ever let herself love anyone because sooner or later they're going to die and she doesn't think she can handle that kind of pressure." He looked up at me in disgust. "Can you believe it, Herb? I mean . . . Jesus H., can you believe it?"

"You are out of your frigging mind, you know," I told him less than tolerantly. "You've been chasing that woman like an idiot since you were both in diapers and she just doesn't want to be bothered, right?"

His expression was glum.

"So I don't get it. Why are you killing yourself?"

He went from glum to suicidal.

"Mike?"

He only sighed.

I wanted to hit him then, put some black around his lights. This was exactly what I did not need tonight, not after Rich yesterday and Mary's confessions on the phone. And it wasn't long before he realized from my silence that he wasn't going to get any of my sympathy, only a strong dose of the truth heavily laced with my own brand of self-pity.

But Jesus, you'd think even a pal like him would understand what was happening to me. He knew. He *knew* what it was like, and he *knew* this was the absolute worst time he could have picked to come crying on my shoulder.

"Well, shit on you," he said at last, pushing himself to his feet. "I'm going for a ride."

"Good. It'll cool you off."

"Like hell. Maybe I'll drive into a telephone pole or a truck or something."

"Not on my block," I said. "I've got work to do."

He gave me a halfhearted finger and stalked off, and a few seconds later I heard a car start and tires squeal as he sped away. Then I felt rotten. He was looking for help and all I did was shove his stupidity down his throat. Jesus, I'd make a hell of a priest; I definitely wasn't being much of a friend.

Then I remembered Mary and went back inside. Locked the door. Pulled aside a stained dropcloth and sat on a stool to look at my project.

It was a tomb.

On that television special I had watched, I'd

been fascinated by the way the rich used to be buried in the real old days—in huge stone tombs with their likenesses carved on the lids. Like Queen Elizabeth I, and Mary, Queen of Scots, and a bunch of other people I had never even heard of. Some of the tombs were so elaborate they were hysterical; others so simple they were stunning. Some effigies had been painted, others retained the stone's natural color; biblical verses, poems, life histories, political lies, were sometimes engraved along the sides; and more than once, a husband and wife were buried together, and together they were carved, as if they were napping.

Nobody did that anymore, and it really was Art if you looked at it kind of sideways, and Danvers sure as hell couldn't deny it was unusual.

So I began with small blocks of wood, a couple of feet long at the most, and tried to create facsimiles of what I had seen, and of the pictures I found in the library at college and in town. I decided after the first few attempts went sour not to have them in fancy clothes, like the Elizabethans, but the way someone might be buried today—in a suit and tie, or a Sunday or birthday dress. Then I thought it would be even better to have them represented the way they were in life—some in jeans, some in tuxedos, some in evening gowns, things like that. I tried a baseball uniform, a cop's outfit and, one night when I was pissed at Uncle Gil, a judge's robes with astrological signs along the hem.

Jesus, they were terrible.

The results looked like what they were—whittling without any force behind them, without any caring. I stopped and did some sketches, but they didn't help either—they looked great, but they were only . . . sketches.

I had started in February.

By the end of the month I was ready to take the bus into Hartford and throw myself into the Connecticut River.

Then I discovered my first solution—I was working too small. The power of the originals lay partly in their size. Life-size. And after a lot of wheedling, of whimpering, of swearing up and down it was a secret and I'd tell as soon as I could, I got Uncle Gil to have a carpenter friend make me a thick block of wood six feet long and five feet high. It took three men to carry it into the shed. It hasn't moved from the spot where they dropped it.

I was scared to death to start because I couldn't afford a single mistake, but one look at my sketches and I knew I couldn't use any of them. Not even now.

And that's when I discovered my second solution, the most obvious one—I needed a real subject to work with, not just some imaginary person.

That's why I couldn't talk to Mary.

I had chosen her to be the model for my corpse.

And there she was now, lying peacefully with those green eyes closed, those soft hands folded on her stomach. Only the effigy was done. The base was still incomplete, because I had no idea what to put there yet. But it was all right, anyway. I mean, you could tell it was her if you knew her—but it wasn't good enough. It wasn't good enough by half, and I had less than two weeks to get it all done.

A car backfired on Raglin and I jumped, grinned at myself and pulled the stool closer, reached out and ran my hands along the lines of her body. She was smooth, cool, and I let my fingers trace the folds and curves of the dress she was wearing, in my mind, the white dress I had seen her in last March, at a concert on campus. Suddenly, I began giggling and couldn't stop. I found myself pressing down on her forehead and whispering, "Heal! Heal!" to her closed eyes, to the mouth slightly parted, standing and pretending I was a tent preacher bringing the wooden dead back to life.

"Heal!" I said loudly, and fell back on the stool, laughing harder and shaking my head.

I was crazy.

I had finally flipped the old lid and had gone totally nuts. If my uncle saw me, he'd probably have the papers signed before he got me back to the house; if my aunt saw me, she'd tsk and fret a lot and tell me I ought to go to a movie or something to clear my head so I could work better.

Maybe they were both right.

I looked at Mary for nearly half an hour, envisioning what I wanted to have there, growing more frustrated by the minute because I didn't know the secret of how to do it. Twice, I picked up a blade and took a sliver off here, a splinter there, and twice put the blade back down before I ruined what little I already had. I did some sanding to smooth imagined rough edges. I dusted her off three or four times. Then another bout of staring, as if by magic I could shift the wood's molecules without moving a muscle. What it did was give me a headache.

"Leave, fool," I ordered myself at last. "Leave, and seek inspiration in a chocolate shake, you jerk."

I stood, replaced the dropcloth and the blade, and switched off the light. Then I went outside, locked the door behind me, and saw someone standing at the corner of the house.

No light from any of the neighbors came through the pines and high shrubs; there was only a dim square of grey-white on the lawn under the kitchen window. Whoever it was stood just beyond its reach, and for a moment I thought it might be that guy Stick was talking about, the guy from the picnic. Then I realized it had to be Mike, back to apologize after his tantrum had run its course.

"Hey," I said, grinning and walking toward him. "Listen, you gotta hear what—"

I stopped.

A sudden, strong gust of wind punched me in the back, making me duck my head and fold my arms tightly over my chest, filling my ears with a high-pitched roaring. And it was cold. Nightcold. It started my teeth chattering, my eyes watering, and, for a frightening second, sucked the strength from my legs. I stumbled, was ready to fall, and the gust passed as quickly as it had come. Blowing like a whale, I rubbed my arms to bring back some warmth and hunched my shoulders sharply to chase away the tightness that had settled across my spine.

"Jesus, Mike, did you feel that? Holy shit, I—"

He was gone.

There was only the kitchen glow, and the flower garden bordered by painted brick.

"Mike?"

I ran to the front and stopped at the gate. The

street was empty, no cars at the curbs, no sound of traffic on Chancellor Avenue, off to my left.

A shudder that was probably a memory of the wind had me holding onto the fence until it passed, and I told myself it was my imagination and what I ought to do was go for a walk to clear my head. And as I did, hands in my pockets and head down, I wondered if it was all just overreacting. I had been grumpy with Aunt May and Stick when they were only trying to help, I'd bitched at Mike when he was only looking for an ear, and I don't think Mary really believed I was sincere about her grief. Maybe, I thought, it's really all me. Maybe I ought to turn around, go home, and get some studying done. It would take my mind off things. It would, as May said, keep me from dwelling too much on the bad stuff, like Rich.

By then I was heading up Centre Street, catching glimpes of this gloomy-looking kid in the shop windows, not paying attention to the people who were walking past me; turning a corner, the clock on the bank striking nine, and going on past the high school, past houses I think I've only seen in the dark, thinking about dying.

I was on the Pike when I finally looked to see where I was heading, standing under the blinking amber light that was supposed to slow traffic before it turned onto Mainland Road. The highway was deserted, the few streetlamps giving it a coat of shimmering black.

I crossed over.

I guess I expected some sort of sign there, an accusing arrow pointing to the spot where Mary had held his head and cried, a flashing red bulb to mark where the stupid bastard had ruined my life because he didn't understand how much more I needed his girl than he did.

There was nothing but gravel that didn't even look disturbed.

I went home.

I went to bed.

I dreamed that my carved Mary walked through the walls and joined me under the covers.

I woke up when Aunt May shook me; I sat up when I saw how pale her face was, and how sad were her eyes.

The hospital reception room was practically empty when I got there. There was an old lady sitting with a little kid who wouldn't stop asking for his mommy, and a guy who looked like he'd be more comfortable sitting in the cab of a truck. The nurse on duty told me there were no visitors. I said thanks, asked for the men's room, and walked around the corner, right into the elevator that took me to the top floor. The station there was deserted, so I went down the hall almost walking on my toes, looking through large windows that showed me mostly old people, lying under clear plastic tents, tubes and wires and monitor screens keeping them out of sight.

And Mike.

In the last room, wrapped like a mummy, both legs in traction, both arms in casts.

"What are you doing here? Visiting hours are over."

In the movies, the guy says he's a brother or a cousin. I didn't say anything. I just looked at him until the nurse took my arm and led me away. She was sorry, she said, but there are rules and did I know him very well. The look on my face shut her up; and when I asked her how he was, the look on her face told me I'd asked a stupid question.

I waited for a while downstairs before going home. I was glad there were clouds because I didn't need spring sunshine to tell me life goes on no matter how lousy you feel; what I did need was a thunderstorm, a strong wind, a cliff overlooking a turbulent sea. What I got was Uncle Gil and Aunt May, sneaking around like I had the plague, smiling sadly, nodding, and keeping themselves so busy I didn't have a chance to ask them to talk.

I called Stick, but he couldn't come to the phone.

I called Mary, but she wasn't there.

I even called Amy, but her mother said she was locked in her room and wouldn't come out. Would I mind coming over to see if I could calm her down?

I hung up without saying goodbye.

Then I went out to the shed and stared at dead Mary, and thought about how some people can go all their lives without having all their friends die on them until they're supposed to, how some people can get through college without having a crisis every ten minutes, about how some people just can't seem to help latching onto someone else, like having a transfusion and all the problems flow from one person to the other, get solved, and flow back and everything's all right—and if it isn't all right, at least it's bearable until next time.

A finger traced the lines of her wooden hair, the lines that soared up and away from her forehead and down around her ears, just like in real life; it stopped to show the way her cheeks were slightly sunken, the way her chin was almost but not quite pointed, the way a muscle on the left side of her neck stood out even when she was resting.

Rich was dead, and I was glad.

Mike was going to die, and all afternoon I worked at some decent tears, some feeling other than a horrid sense of relief that I wouldn't have to listen to his constant bitching anymore about a woman only a year out of high school who wouldn't give him the right time of day.

I thought he was my friend, and I thought I should cry.

I knew something was wrong with me, but I didn't know what, and I didn't know then whether or not to be scared.

I slept in my bed, but I dreamed I was in Mary's, made of cloud and soft rain and warm sunlight and her; I slept so soundly that Aunt May had to wake me, and remind me that in less than two hours I had my first exam.

I don't think I ever moved so damned fast in my life. I skipped my shower, skipped breakfast, and couldn't believe it when I ran the whole two miles to Hawksted's small campus. I was, barely, on time; luckily, English still remained my best subject and the professor my easiest mark—the questions were simple, the conclusions to be drawn obvious, and I was one of the first to turn my work in.

As planned, Stick met me at the student union. We found an empty lounge and dropped onto one of the couches, doing our act about misery and woe and how God Himself would have to grade the papers with divine compassion before we could pass. And when that was done, we matched schedules for the rest of the week. My next test was

Wednesday morning, the first of a string of three in a row. Stick had one a day, the fortunes of war.

Then he told me about Mike.

"Jackass wrapped his old man's car around a telephone pole, can you believe it? He must have been doing ninety, the cops said." He shook his head, took off his baseball cap, and slapped his knee with it. "I don't get it, y'know? He just doesn't do stuff like that, speeding and crap."

I was cold in that room, and I couldn't meet his eyes.

"You go see him?"

I nodded. "I tried, anyway. Snuck up when they weren't looking, but they caught me."

"Yeah. He looks—"

I glared, and he didn't say it, and whatever we were going to do that afternoon was instantly replaced by a trip to the hospital, he on his new moped and me riding behind. It was a tight squeeze, and he laughed most of the way because our combined weights held us down to barely a walk.

"Damn good thing you're dropping some tonnage," he told me as we walked into the building. "Christ, the way you used to be, you would have squashed it flat."

I shoved him hard through the revolving doors, sneered at his protest, then composed myself as I approached the receptionist and asked about Mike

Buller. She looked at me kind of funny, looked at Stick until he took off his cap, and looked pointedly between us into the waiting room. I half turned and saw a group of people gathered around Mike's parents—his mother was crying, his father looked ready to tear the place apart.

"Shit," Stick said, grabbed a tissue from a box on the desk, and blew his nose.

"I'm going," I told him when he started to walk over.

"What?" He stopped and slapped his cap back on. "But you can't, Herb! You gotta . . . you gotta say something, don't you think?"

I shrugged. I supposed I did, but I didn't know what, and I wasn't going to get myself into that mess over there, standing around with my hands in my pockets while I watched the Bullers' world fall apart.

"C'mon," Stick said, reaching for my arm.

I stepped away and told him no with a look.

"Sometimes," he said then, "you are really a shit, Herb, you know?"

I ignored him and left, walked up to the luncheonette and ordered a chocolate shake. It tasted lousy, but I sat at the counter anyway, like I was in a bar and nursing a drink. I stayed for an hour and had a sandwich I didn't finish, took a walk through the park and watched some kids playing ball, then wandered again until I passed Station Motors and saw myself in the window.

The first thing I thought was, there was someone standing behind me, that damned guy again—but when I looked, I was alone. And when I looked back, I saw this almost skinny guy, this blond-haired guy wearing baggy pants and a baggy shirt, with eyes, because of the dark car in the front of the showroom, that looked like empty holes.

I put a hand to the plate glass as if I could touch myself, backed away to the curb, and looked down at myself. My hands began to tremble. My stomach felt ready to get rid of the shake and sandwich. I must have stood there for nearly five minutes, pulling at my shirt, pulling my waistband away from my gut, acting like I'd never seen myself before.

I knew I hadn't been eating right for a while; I knew that I'd been swearing to go on a real, honest-to-god diet if that's what it would take to be human again; and I knew that the last time I'd said that was only Friday afternoon. When we were all at the orchard.

But you can't lose fifty pounds in three days.

You just can't.

Another stare at the window, another look at my

stomach, and I started to run. I was scared. A million names of real and fake diseases tumbled over each other in their attempts to explain, and a million other reasons sounded just as bad.

You can't lose fifty pounds in three days.

You just can't, and expect to live.

When I got home, everyone was gone, there was no note, and I could smell a full turkey dinner cooking and baking in the kitchen. I didn't go in. I ran upstairs to the bathroom, stripped off my clothes, and stood in front of the full-length mirror on the door.

"God," I said. "God, Jesus, what . . ."

Not only wasn't I fat like I used to be, there wasn't even any sagging. My skin was normal, no folds where the weight used to be, no wattles on my neck, no creases . . . no nothing.

"Oh, god. Oh, Jesus."

I sat on the floor, trying to get a breath and stop the tears that were there suddenly, then grabbing onto my arms, my legs, to keep them from shaking themselves right out of their sockets.

I felt the cold, but I was used to it.

And I heard the buzzing in my ears, the murmuring of a thousand voices so low I couldn't understand them.

And I looked at myself again and something heaved in my stomach; I crawled over to the toilet, threw up the lid, and leaned over the bowl. But nothing came out because there was nothing inside, and the retching went on so long I started to whimper at the pain, at the burning, at the tiny flecks of black I saw floating in the water.

I don't think I've cried so much since I was a baby.

I could smell turkey and bread dressing and hot rolls and fresh butter.

The light dimmed before I was able to move again, and the first thing I did was put my clothes back on, not caring how I looked, only wondering who I could go to, who I could find who would tell me what was wrong.

The second thing I did was smash the mirror with everything I could pull from the medicine cabinet.

The house was dark.

I could smell pumpkin pie and ice cream and whipped cream and fresh cider.

I stumbled into the living room and stared at the phone.

I couldn't call Mike, I couldn't call Rich, I couldn't call Amy because she would only want to talk about how her life was over.

Mary wasn't home.

Stick was.

"What do you want," he said flatly.

"Stick, I'm in trouble, man, real trouble."

He didn't say anything, and it didn't hit me right away that he was still pissed about my leaving the hospital without talking to Mike's folks.

"Stick, honest to god, I think I'm in big trouble."

"No shit," he said, his voice oddly slurred. "But in case you hadn't noticed, friend, some of us other guys got troubles, too. You just don't seem to care anymore."

If he had been in the room, I would have knocked out his teeth. "Stick, you don't get it, man. I—"

"I ain't got the time," he said then. "I just slashed my wrists."

"Jesus, that isn't funny, Stick." There was no response. "Stick? Stick, goddamnit, I said that isn't—" The receiver dropped on his end and I could hear it swinging back and forth, slamming against something, hollow and loud. "Stick! Jesus, Stick!"

If the front door hadn't opened right away, I think I would have smashed right through it.

Two blocks, two long and hard blocks, and I jumped the stairs to Reese's porch and started pounding on the door. No one answered. I yelled, I rang the doorbell, I ran to the windows that looked in on the front room, cursing because the curtains were drawn, finally finding a crack wide enough to look through.

He was there. I could see his feet poking out of the foyer, I could see the receiver swinging from its cord and hitting the wall, and I could see on one knee what looked like blood.

I know what I should have done. I know I should have busted a window and called the police, or gone to a neighbor's and begged for help. But I ran instead, like I'd killed him myself, staying to the shadows, ducking behind poles and trees and even hedges when a car went by, turning around whenever I saw someone walking toward me.

By the time I ran out of wind and my legs had started to scream, it was twilight.

Soft colors, soft breeze.

And I was in the orchard.

I'm not a coward, you know. I know when to fight and when to back off. But when I looked around and realized where I was, I couldn't stop myself from wishing my mother was here.

Most of the trees were dead. Gnarled, tall, without the grace of a tombstone to lend them some purpose. Their rows were ragged, their trunks bent and angled, and the shadows they cast were like no shadows I've ever seen. They were cold, and the air around touched with the feel of a ghost or a bad dream. The grass grew, but not high; there were weeds without blossoms; the rocks were small, the stones sharp; and the dead leaves blown in here from the woods to the north were always brittle, and bladed, even after it rained.

I didn't like it here, didn't know why I'd come when I should have been with Mary, or Aunt May, or even Uncle Gil.

Anyone who could tell me what the hell was going on.

Twilight deepened to dusk.

I turned to leave, holding my stomach and deciding that maybe I should be in the hospital. The doctors there would know what was wrong with me; they would listen to my problems and they'd cure me, really cure me. They'd take me apart and put me back together, and when I got out I'd be just as good as new.

The thought made me smile, and with one hand out to push away the branches, I took one step, and saw Mary's tomb.

It was lying in a clear space, like an aisle between rows of trees, and when it registered that I wasn't seeing things, that I wasn't losing my mind, I started to lose my temper, to search for a name to put blame to for playing this sick joke as I ran over and dropped beside it, leaning close because the light was going fast and I wanted to be sure it hadn't been hurt.

"Jesus," I said.

"Jesus!" I shouted, and jumped to my feet, fists ready, teeth bared, daring the goddamned bastards to come out of hiding and face me like men.

The pastels faded and shaded to black.

Something moved.

I froze, even though I wasn't sure I'd heard anything, a hand out over Mary as if to protect her.

Then it moved again, just off to my left.

I looked up at the twisted branches and they were hands reaching for my scalp; I backed away from the boles that were scaled black on the sides as if marked by a great fire; I stumped over a rock half buried in the ground and told myself that if I didn't stop it, I was going to scare myself to death.

A twig snapped.

A foot scuffed through dead leaves.

I turned quickly, breath ice in my throat, and saw nothing, saw no one, not even my shadow.

"Who the hell is it?" I demanded, amazed that my voice didn't crack. "Is this your idea of a joke? Is it? Well, it ain't goddamned funny!"

Far behind me, on the highway, a truck sounded its horn.

A soft voice in front, a whispering, words I couldn't make out.

"All right, knock it off. You think it's funny? You know Stick is dead? Huh? Do you bastards know Stick is dead?"

Something flew overhead, low and banking sharply, and I ducked, lifted a shoulder, and waved a frantic hand to drive it away. It came by again, wings short and chopping the air, dropping me to one knee while I tried to move backward. A third time, and it was gone, black into black, leaving me panting and feeling incredibly stupid.

"Idiot," I muttered as I struggled to stand. It was only a bat, after a bug I couldn't see. Feeling like a class-A jerk, I dusted my jeans off, rolled my shoulders, and moved over to Mary to see how I was going to get the tomb back home. I figured they must have used a truck; they must have broken the lock on the shed and carried her out in a pickup.

But I didn't know anyone who owned one, and no one, not even Stick, had known what I was doing.

It's a dream, I told myself then; it's nothing but a stupid dream and you're going to wake up any minute now. Any minute now you're going to get out of bed and go down to breakfast and tell Aunt May you're on another diet. And Stick will be there, telling you you're an asshole because you won't give up Mary.

I stood over her image and shook my head,

reaching out to touch her, and yanking my hand back when I felt the cold wood. Looked up to the moon—it was new, just a crescent, but it and its stars were bright enough to let me see the lines in Mary's face, and the shadow by the tree.

It wasn't Stick Reese, because he was dead.

It wasn't Mike, and it wasn't Richard, and it wasn't Uncle Gil.

And it certainly wasn't Mary, come to bring me to her bed.

There was little form, less substance; there was no movement at all. In a gap between trees, only vague ripplings in black to show it was there at all, the suggestions of a dress or cloak, the outline of a covered head.

When the breeze gusted, it swayed.

And it appeared to be listening.

I cleared my throat, wiped my mouth, and tried real hard not to think about psychotic ax- and knife-wielding killers who preyed on innocent college juniors, slashing their throats and leaving them in deserted fields and orchards to be found days later, picked to pieces by the crows.

I looked over my shoulder, figuring the distance to the road and the odds of my being able to get there safely, assuming I didn't fall, assuming I wasn't caught.

The moon touched the orchard with traces of

dead silver; the wind touched the air with traces of screams.

I eased back a step and looked to the shadow to see if it had followed.

It hadn't.

It just stood there.

I thought about claiming I wasn't alone, my friends were here with me and there was no chance it could take me without getting hurt itself; I thought about claiming I had a gun and wouldn't hesitate to use it.

Standing there.

Sweat dropped into my eyes. I shook my head, rubbed a hand over my face, and looked again to see how much closer it had gotten.

It hadn't.

It was gone.

Panic tightened my groin. My fingers clenched, stiffened, clenched again as I turned a quick tight circle, staring into the dark, looking for the shadow, finally closing my eyes and releasing a breath in a barely audible moan. Christ, I thought; and I punched my chest once, punishment for the way my imagination had scared me. I was alone. I knew it. Because everyone else had left me.

"All right," I said briskly, clapping my hands and giving myself a shake. "All right, let's get moving here, huh, Johns? Let's get our ass in gear.''

First I'd take care of Mary, then get to the hospital and take care of myself.

Slowly I walked around the huge block of wood, peering closely again to be doubly sure nothing had been damaged. It was hard, though. I kept hearing things behind me, feeling things watching, feeling the nightcold as it sifted down from the moon. I knelt at the head, at each side, and finally the foot, suddenly awfully tired and holding onto the top corners when I pushed myself up.

And looked at my thin hands, at the thin pale shadow that draped over Mary.

I don't know what happened, but I felt really dizzy and fell forward, my hands landing on either side of Mary's hips to keep me from landing on her, one knee cracking against the rim.

The top moved.

The wind whispered.

I eased myself away so carefully I almost cramped, knowing something was wrong because that wasn't any top—it was all one big piece, with nothing inside.

I reached out, pulled back, dried my hands on my jeans, and reached out again like I was ready to put my whole hand in fire. Mary, I thought; Mary, please help me. And I pushed a corner, hard. Nothing happened, and I laughed dryly. So I pushed a second time—and the scrape of wood against wood dropped me to my knees. I looked up and saw the shadows standing under the trees. I looked down and saw white bone gleaming through my skin.

Then I pushed the corner again, just enough to see that the wood block was hollow.

And I heard myself screaming as I leaned over, and looked in.

I don't care for the dark, but I think now it protects me.

Just as I think that whatever lives in the orchard has turned everything around, and somehow filled me the day I ran through it so I couldn't take any more—Mike's worries about Amy, Stick's rotten home, even Rich's silent gloating over the prize he thought he'd won.

And my own troubles, most of them minor though I wouldn't believe it.

Whatever it is, it filled me with emptiness, and I cast emptiness back.

They'll never find the car that killed Richard, or learn why Mike lost control and Stick used a razor.

I pretended to care, and they knew I was lying and couldn't escape the cold I gave them in return.

And Mary, my Mary with the flaming red hair, would probably run if I tried to explain and showed her the tomb and all the letters I never sent her that I keep in my drawer.

She would run, she would hate me . . . unless Aunt May is wrong and there are real miracles after all, and Mary, my Mary, would see how much I hurt and know how to save me from the dark in the orchard.

I can only wait to find out.

I can only lie beneath her image to stay away from the cold, out there, in the shadows, and pray that my clothes aren't more baggy still, that I really can feel flesh still clinging to my bones . . . and pray even harder that the darkform in my arms that I use for a bed and pillow is only a dream slowly rotting to nightmare.

I can only wait, and be patient.

For my Mary's asleep.

I know.

I hear her breathing.

Part Two

I See Her Sweet and Fair

Rising like a nightflower against the full of the moon, lifting slowly to a grey silhouette . . .

Brett saw the light from the living room window and almost jumped from the chair in his haste to avoid it. Ice spiderwalked his spine, his palms grew moist, and when he licked at his lips, he felt them dry and cracking.

It's only the moon, idiot, he told himself harshly; it's only the damned moon.

But he pulled the shade down so quickly it snapped up again, rattled around the roller, cord and grip cracking sharp against the pane. He grabbed for the woven loop, cursed when it rapped his knuckle, and finally trapped it in both hands. A deep breath. A sigh. He lowered the shade a second time and held it until he was sure it wouldn't fly free again.

He knew he was being foolish, but it was increasingly something he couldn't fight off. The light the moon dropped on the carpet unnerved him, and though he ordered himself to stop behaving like a child, he couldn't help a glance into each of the corners. His eyes closed briefly; his lungs filled with a breath that he held until his hands finally stopped their trembling. Then he turned away from the window, took his chair by the hearth, and picked up the newspaper where he'd dropped it just before.

The headlines were familiar, as were the stories below them. He looked for the comics, but they didn't amuse him; he scanned the sports section, but knew none of the teams; he tried to decipher the stock market for nearly ten minutes, giving up with a grunt when his eyes started to water.

A book was next, jammed between the cushion and the armrest. He couldn't remember where he'd left off, so he skimmed until he discovered something unfamiliar. After three pages he put it back down—the names meant nothing, and he had no idea why they were saying those things about one another.

The television was broken.

The radio was in the kitchen.

And his son was out with Evelyn Zayer, a girl who spent more time on the telephone than any forty he had ever known. Leslie, when he wasn't complaining about Brett's refusal to let him have an apartment of his own, laughingly called his good looks the family curse; Brett only hoped the boy would remember to finish his education and not run off to get married, and leave him alone.

An hour, and he kept glancing over his shoulder at the shade, at the dark window. *Seeing the girl standing—*

"Jesus, will you stop it, for god's sake?"

He got up, slapped the back of the chair and strolled into the kitchen, switched on the light and opened the refrigerator. His stomach told him he had better eat something soon or he'd start in earnest with the snacks and blow his diet all to hell. But nothing he saw appealed to him, nothing prompted his taste buds to wake up and demand. The cupboards were the same, and so was the pantry.

"But I'm hungry," he insisted.

No, you're not, you're bored, he answered with

a sour grin, and decided to cure it by getting the hell out and going for a walk.

He took his windbreaker from the hall closet, turned on a few lights in case Les came home before he did, and left, testing the door twice to be sure it was locked. Another grin, this one quick and bright, and he stepped down to the walk, looked up at the moon.

Out here, under the elm that had taken over the front yard, it seemed perfectly normal. Huge, almost white; and he couldn't understand why something so lovely had bothered him tonight, and had bothered him every night for at least the past week.

Not true, he thought then; not true at all.

He could mark the moment it began from the first time he had seen his son in what they used to call action.

It was last Friday, and he had taken Denise Quarell to the movies, to the Regency Theater, newly constructed on an old parking lot east of the Mariner Cove. It was a beautiful place, in brick and white trim, and the only indication it was a theater at all was the ticket booth in front. There was no marquee, no posters, the walls flanking the entrance broken only by curtained windows that looked into the lobby.

After the show ended, he had waited for her on the sidewalk, smoking a cigarette and watching with quiet amusement the other customers leaving. There were, in his eavesdropping, the usual arguments and discussions about the film, the refreshments, the price of a babysitter, the time someone promised a mother to be home, July's weather, school, and work. Then, as he turned away to drop his cigarette into the gutter, he heard his son pleading with a girl not to be that way, for god's sake, it was only a movie and why shouldn't he appreciate what he was seeing?

"And I suppose you weren't appreciating that hulk in the jockstrap."

"Well, for god's sake, he's a man!"

They passed him, and he turned his head just enough to see them, hip to hip, heads together, the girl gesturing angrily with both hands. He stared at her back, then looked away and closed his eyes, trying to bring a name to the short brown hair, the slender body, the voice that sounded too young for her age. He snapped his fingers just as Denise joined him.

"You call?" she said.

"Amy," he said.

"No, Denise," she told him, half turned him and grinned. "Do you remember me? I'm your date."

He laughed. "No, not you."

Frowning, she stepped back with hands on her hips. "Not me? You mean you're out with two women tonight? Is that where you went when you said you were going to the men's room, right in the middle of the nude scene?"

The tease was there, in her eyes, in the set of her lips, and he felt himself blushing. He hadn't left because of the naked woman, though he supposed his timing could have been better.

She saw how flustered he was and laughed quietly, slipped her arm through his and started them walking. "What, if I may ask, were you talking about?"

"Them." And he pointed quickly at his son and the girl now a full block away. "I just remembered her name."

"You could have asked me."

"You know her?"

"Sure." They passed the Mariner, forgetting for the moment their after-film drink. "She comes to the bank at least once a week. A regular savings demon. The worst I ever saw." She thought for a moment. "That stuff last May. The boy who was killed in the car accident?"

He snapped his fingers again. "Yeah, right! Gus Buller's kid. She was—"

"His girlfriend," she said. "So they say, anyway. They also say, if it hadn't been for what Les did, she probably would have killed herself."

He only grunted. Les was no genius, had no special artistic talents, but somehow he had developed the means to communicate well with people near his own age. He had met Amy Niles once or twice before, and after her boyfriend had died, he had spent a lot of time with her, talking, walking, getting her to go out and start living again.

Brett was damned proud of the boy; he only wished he knew how to tell him how he felt.

They had stopped talking then, had walked on in companionable silence until he realized they were on the last block before Mainland road, and Les and Amy were running across it to the slope and field beyond.

"Uh-oh." Denise yanked him to a halt. "This, Father dear, is as far as we go."

They made an abrupt and clumsy about-face, giggling as they hurried back up the street, creating several definitely unpleasant scenarios that would be played out very loudly in public when his son turned around, saw him, and accused his father of being his shadow.

"You would not be long for this world," Denise had told him.

He had tried not to laugh when she pinched his waist, ducked away from a slap when he pinched her back—and ended up facing east, just as Les and the girl reached the top of the slope on the other side of the road. His son was already pushing through a gap in the bramble hedge; Amy had turned to face the village.

She was caught beyond the reach of any streetlamp, and the trees on Mainland's eastern side blocked any house light from spilling across.

But the moon that night was high, and it gave her silver light, seemed to touch only her and not the brush around her.

She saw him.

He knew she saw him.

And he didn't have to be any closer to see the look on her face—only a year or so older than Les, but at the moment, before Denise had grabbed his arm and pulled him on, he would have sworn she was a hag, less out of the movies than out of a bad dream.

Then a cloud hid the moon, and she vanished in black.

Foolish, he thought now as he reached the end of the block and moved on; the kids had only been doing what he himself never had the nerve to do, and Denise had finally teased him back to the Mariner Lounge with promises of free drinks.

But the moon, and the look . . .

Remembering how his next few nights had been filled with shadowed dreams. He had been unable to call them back when he woke in the morning, but the sweat on the sheets, the clammy feel of his skin, let him know what he'd been through, even if he hadn't understood.

It was the look, and the moon, and, he supposed, an aftermath of the murder.

A week ago, the day after he'd seen Les and Amy. A young girl, a close friend of his son's. Brett had met her and hadn't much liked her, as he hadn't liked any of the girls Les went out with these days. They were too modern for his taste, too forward, too blunt. Though he knew that someday one of those young women would take the boy away, he hoped Les had more brains than glands and wouldn't be fooled until he was good and ready.

He turned another corner, heading nowhere in particular, and realized suddenly he was listening to the night, for the sounds he'd been hearing—footsteps, quiet footsteps, just within range, the maker just out of sight.

He told himself it was only caution, natural in a cop, and it was, after all, only someone else strolling around a near corner, the summer night air carrying the tread and muffling it.

Someone else. Nothing more.

It wasn't Amy; it wasn't the moon.

Thirty minutes later, still wandering, he felt an unseasonal chill seep through his jacket. He held his arms closer to his sides, hunched his shoulders a bit, and looked around to get his bearings. A lopsided smile. He was on Denise's street and wasn't surprised, rather hoped as he sped up that it was some sort of omen, or a signal from his unconscious that he wasn't nuts, only lonely.

"Aw, poor fella," he said, laughing at himself as he turned into her yard.

She lived in a small two-bedroom cottage squeezed between two large mock-Tudors whose hedges seemed determined to absorb the smaller house. He took the slate walk at a run, took the steps to the porch in a single leap, and had his finger on the doorbell before he could change his mind.

She opened the door as if she'd been waiting.

"Hi!" he said brightly, thinking glumly that even Leslie could be more clever than that.

She was pleased to see him, it was obvious, but she was also puzzled. The freckles across her forehead almost vanished in a frown, while the dimples on her cheeks deepened when finally she smiled.

"Well, hi. You selling something?"

A jerk of his head over his shoulder. "A walk?

It's a nice night. We could stop for a burger someplace. Maybe catch the late show? It's a spy story, I think.''

She laughed and waved him in. "Hey, Brett, don't you believe in telephones?''

It wasn't a refusal, but here, in this house crowded with furniture and soft lights, he felt abruptly claustrophobic. The unease must have showed, because she grabbed a sweater quickly from the newel post and took his arm.

"Lead on, good-lookin'. Tonight I'm all yours.''

Halfway down the block in silence, and she tugged at his arm. "Something the matter?''

Her hair was short and auburn, her face and figure round, and in her jeans and sweater she looked a full decade younger than his own thirty-nine.

"Something bothering you, cop?''

He denied it with a shake of his head. "Just restless. I took a chance you were home." He winked. "I got lucky.''

"You sure did. I was supposed to spend the weekend in Hartford, at some stupid banking conference. I changed my mind at the last minute because, don't you know, bankers are so damned boring.''

She was an officer in the Savings and Loan on Centre Street, destined it was said for the presidency one of these days. That surprised him. Most bankers he had known in the past were singularly conservative, and Denise definitely was not of the same mold; they also grew cautious the more time they spent behind the desk, and if anything, she was even more enthusiastic than the day she'd first walked through the door. All that energy was amazing to him, and he didn't know where she got it.

"Me, too," she said.

"Huh?"

"I can't for the life of me figure out what hold all that money has over me." She turned away, but he saw the smile. "I guess I'm just naturally greedy."

"Right."

"I mean, it's dirty, you know. That money is absolutely filthy."

"Sure."

"You wouldn't believe what I look like when I get home."

"I know."

She stopped, made him turn. "Brett, I'll enjoy the burgers, and I'll enjoy the film, and I'll probably enjoy the conversation, too, once I get used to being fed one word at a time."

He rubbed his temple, his chin, and felt more than a bit silly. "Sorry."

They walked again and decided on the luncheonette for their meal. And as they ate, he found

himself responding to the most innocuous questions with baleful stories of his life, particularly
how he had married Grace Black when they were
juniors in college, had Les a year later, and little
Alice five years after that.

"Too young," he said. "Once we grew up, we
grew apart."

Three years ago, Grace had left him, with Alice. And on the road to her mother's a truck had
skidded, and the car she was driving slammed into
it, and under.

He closed his eyes, set his mouth.

"How did Les take it?"

"I don't know. Really." He chuckled and raised
an eyebrow. "In the beginning, he wouldn't let go
of me for fear I'd leave him too. Now it seems to
be the other way around. I can't let go, and he
wants his own place."

She gave him a look he didn't quite understand.
"You have to let go, Brett, you know. Sooner or
later, you'll have to let go."

"Yeah. But . . . yeah."

A long silence made him uncomfortable, made
him think about living in that suddenly big house
all alone.

"You ever consider getting married again?" she
asked.

"It's crossed my mind."

"Three years is a long time these days."

"You're right. But I have Les to think of, too."

He paid the check and they walked down to the theater.

"You love him, don't you."

He looked at her, puzzled. "Of course. Did you ever think I didn't? I mean, don't I show it?"

She wrinkled her nose at him. "Yes, if you're worried about it. I was just asking."

Funny question, he thought, but said nothing more, though it kept coming back, even during the film. It made him nervous. Was she proposing? He had a curious feeling that one more word, one pleasant look, and she would think he was accepting. When he squirmed, she kissed his cheek and told him to knock it off before she called the usher and had him thrown out.

And later, in the lobby, he walked over to the concession counter to get a pack of cigarettes, turned, and saw her talking to a woman a bit taller than she, white-blonde hair, tight jeans, and snug blouse. He swore silently and wished there was a back exit handy, forced a smile on his lips when they saw him and waved.

Victoria Redding, the only policewoman on the force. He had taken her out several times over the past winter, enjoyed himself, and beyond their meetings at the station, hadn't seen much of her since. From a large farm in Vermont, she fit right into village life with scarcely a ripple, and he was surprised when he wondered why he hadn't taken her out again.

"Brett!" she said happily when he joined them, and made no bones about giving him a kiss that lasted a fraction longer than politeness required. "You like the picture?"

He talked at such length that the women started laughing, and he realized with a swallow how nervous he was, how he'd been expecting her to say something like, "Where have you been?" or "Call me sometime," and then have to answer while Denise was listening.

It bothered him, too, that he almost wished she would.

They chatted as they walked outside; Vicky kissed him again quickly and headed for home, claiming early shift the next day. He watched her walk away, then took Denise's hand and went in the opposite direction.

"She always like that?" she asked at last.

"Like what?"

"Like every other word being 'shift' and 'apprehension' and 'busts' and stuff like that."

His smile was wry. "She's trying hard, Denise, she really is. It isn't easy being a woman cop in a small town like this, no matter where she came from. I think, sometimes, me and Stockton are the only ones who like her.''

''That's discrimination.''

He shrugged. ''Maybe. But some of the guys are too old to change and don't trust her, and some of them just think she ought to go around naked.''

A half a block later: ''And you?''

''I'm too old, and she'd look great naked.''

She slapped his arm, hard, and it was difficult to produce a laugh to show her he knew she was kidding.

They turned off the avenue and he slipped off his jacket. The temperature had begun to rise, and there was fog growing in the trees—little more than a thin mist now, just enough to haze the light and set dew on the grass.

When they passed his house, the car wasn't in the drive. He said nothing, but his hand tightened on her arm, and he watched the length of the street as casually as he could despite a silent order to stop worrying about the boy.

''It must be hard,'' she said quietly when they'd moved on.

''Hard?''

''Seeing that girl last week. The one who was killed, I mean. And having Leslie.''

He nodded. It was. It was damned hard, and he could tell she wanted him to talk about it, share some of it, ease the concern by shifting some of the burden. But he couldn't. He had, over the course of their friendship, told her virtually everything else, but trying to explain what it was like to be a parent would have to wait—because she couldn't know, she couldn't possibly know how it felt whenever his son walked out of the house and left him alone.

Victoria understood, he thought then, with a suddenness that confused him, made him frown. Her own son lived with his father in California. But the difference there was, that boy had left and hadn't returned.

On the porch they kissed goodnight, but he sensed it wasn't the same as it had been other times.

Denise, and Victoria.

Y'know, he told himself on the way home, you could wind up in a hell of a lot of trouble, pal, if you don't watch your step.

But was he ready for another wife? And if he was, would it be her?

He paused in midstep; for a disconcerting moment he didn't know which woman he meant.

"Oh, boy," he whispered, not sure if he felt pleased or on edge. "Oh, boy, Brett, you're asking for it now."

He turned left at the corner, listening to his

shoes on the pavement, listening to the nightbirds stir through the mist, slowing three doors from home when he found himself listening to something walking behind him.

Quiet steps, muffled, as the mist thickened to fog and sifted down across his face, making his skin feel clammy, making his shirt feel as if it had just been washed and not dried.

Arrhythmically, then in cadence.

Just as they had been on all the other nights.

He didn't turn around; he didn't sense imminent danger. But that didn't prevent him from stopping at his front walk and reaching down to flick a dead leaf off the flagstone while he looked back up the street and saw nothing but the fog blowing through the streetlight.

Nice move, cop, he thought as he hurried to the steps and took them two at a time; nothing like being a little obvious, huh?

He was reaching for his keys when he heard them again, and this time knew he was wrong; this time there was someone out there who didn't like him at all.

He spun around, dropping into a crouch, his jacket slipping with a hiss to the damp porch floor.

The walk was empty; there was no one in the yard.

Nerves, he decided when he finally went inside.

Those women have got you thinking about things you'd best forget. He poured himself a drink and looked out the window, shuddering when he saw the moon glowing in the mist, nearly dropping the glass when the night filled with sirens.

Rising like a nightflower against the full of the moon, lifting slowly to a grey silhouette that raised its head high, that held its forelegs still, that turned a red eye to the land spread below and listened for the sound that would signal its charge . . .

On Monday morning, Brett decided he was going to run away and join the Foreign Legion. He knew, he just knew this was going to be one of those days.

The Saturday night sirens had only been a signal for a fire on the Pike, but the state of his nerves had him call Denise for an hour's mindless talk. And no sooner had he hung up than Victoria had called; she'd been looking at a picture of her son and needed to hear someone's voice. Another hour passed, and he met her for lunch the next day, and took a Sunday stroll in the park. Not once did she ask him how Leslie was doing. Not once did he feel guilty about not being with Denise.

And last night, he'd been up late, waiting for his son, who had insisted that going out on a Sunday wasn't the end of the world; besides, he was only going to do some studying with Evelyn. Brett had paid for the permission with unaccountable worry, but Les on his return hadn't been sympathetic. He accused his father loudly of not trusting him, of treating him like a child, that it was bad enough having a cop in the family, and now he couldn't even walk in the door without having his whereabouts questioned.

"For god's sake, Dad, when the hell are you gonna ease up?" He had clenched his fists, and he looked ready to cry. "She's right, you know. She really is. I ought to get a place of my own where I could at least have some peace."

"Who's right? Who are you talking about?"

"None of your business," Les snapped. "Just leave me alone."

The outburst had been a shock, and the "she" could only be Evelyn Zayer.

This morning, Les had gone to school early, without saying goodbye.

Yeah, he thought, the Foreign Legion sounds great. Sand and camels and no kids to figure out.

Pushing away from the desk, daring those who passed his office to come in and annoy him, he rubbed his forehead with the heel of one hand, trying to drive off a headache that had lodged there since he'd wakened. It felt like someone had tied an iron clamp around his head and now, in malicious delight, was trying to crush his skull without crushing his brain.

"Gilman," he said to the beaded glass on the door, "you are in bad shape. Real bad shape."

The telephone rang three times before he picked up the receiver, listened for a moment, and returned it to the cradle.

"Please, God," he said as he reached for his sport jacket, "please, let it be a simple breaking and entering, with lots of fingerprints and footprints and the guy's wallet at the scene. C'mon, God, how about it?"

He didn't need a car. He crossed Chancellor Avenue, hurried past the Mariner Cove, and cut through the parking lot to a small blacktopped area behind the Regency Theater. Two patrolmen were standing near the building's corner, keeping a handful of people from going in back; a third met him as he approached.

"What is it, Nick?" he said, already feeling his stomach tighten, his throat begin to dry.

Officer Lonrow, his face blotched and his hands quivering, only pointed behind him.

The theater's back wall was unbroken by any doors, and in its center squatted a large green dumpster whose lid had been thrown up against the brick. Brett started for it, and hesitated when he saw a hand dangling over the side. A young hand. One silver band. A silver bracelet. A thread of dried blood from the hump of one knuckle.

He stopped for a moment and drew his lips between his teeth with a hiss, took several deep breaths, and listened to a woman moaning, a man's voice raised in excited curiosity, a car grinding gears as it turned a far corner.

Then he took a look inside, blinked, and turned away as slowly as he could. Lonrow joined him, and they studied the thick line of trees that separated the theater from the houses behind.

"How did you find her?" he asked.

"Just doing my rounds, as usual," the younger man said between harsh clearings of his throat. "I saw the lid up and was going to close it when I saw . . . the hand. I called you right away."

"Do you know who she is?"

Lonrow shook his head. "Do you?"

"Yeah," he said. "Evelyn Zayer. She's . . . she was a friend of my son's."

"Oh, boy," the man said, but Brett made no comment, only poked into the trees and held his breath when he saw indentations that might have been footprints. He knelt, frowned and squinted, and could find only two, with maybe a third. They were clearly not made by shoes or bare feet, and faint as they were on the hard ground and fallen needles, they could have been made by anything from a dog to a prowling cat. He wasn't surprised; why the hell should things get easy now?

He stood with a groan and waited for the forensic crew to get to work. As soon as he was no longer needed, he let a patrol car take him to the hospital, to the morgue in the basement, where he saw Evelyn's body on a polished metal table. There was a wound in the center of her chest, wide and passing completely through to the spine. He had already heard all the theories on possible weapons after the first girl had died—a sword, an ice pick, a dowel, a stump of wood. But he kept them to himself while he spoke with the girl's parents, forcing himself to remain calm while the mother wailed and the father railed and he saw in their eyes Leslie's name flashing with unmentioned suspicion.

When at last he returned to his office, he slammed the door loudly enough to tell the others he wasn't to be disturbed. But he could still hear the sounds, still see the shadows that passed down the hall. Several times he told himself to get up, get his coat, and go home. It was well after five; there was nothing more he could do here, not today. He had already called Callum Davidson, the theater's manager, and was told that the last of the previous evening's trash had been put in the dumpster just after midnight. There had been no one in the parking lot, no one on the streets.

And he stared at the desk until his eyes began to blur, and all he could think of was Les's temper the night before.

An hour later, he started and cursed when the telephone rang, snapped an angry "Hello," and slumped back in his chair when he heard Denise's voice.

"Sorry," he said wearily. "It's been lousy today."

"Don't worry about it," she said. "I heard."

"Oh."

"Are you okay?"

His smile was halfhearted. "That seems to be your favorite question these days."

"What's your answer this time?"

"Rotten," he admitted.

"Have you . . . what does Les say?"

Suddenly there was heat climbing fast to his cheeks, heat on his palm when he slapped the desk and stood up, heat that blurred through his vision and made him reach blindly for the back of his chair.

"What the hell does Les . . . Jesus, it must be all over town, right? Cop's son suspected of double murder?"

"Brett, wait—"

110

"Christ Almighty!" He knew he was yelling, and he couldn't lower his voice. "Why the hell isn't anyone talking about a teacher, for god's sake, or whatshisname up at the luncheonette? They see these kids every day too, you know. You think these girls are nuns or something? You think Les is the only kid in the world who takes them out?"

"Brett, please!"

He took the receiver from his ear and cradled it gently, his arm rigid with the need to slam it down instead. Then he stalked out of the office, and got as far as the front desk when a voice turned him around.

"You'll have to talk with your boy," Stockton told him quietly, looking as if he wished he were anywhere but here.

Brett clenched his fists, but could do nothing else but nod.

The chief scratched his neck thoughtfully, took a breath, and spat dryly. "I don't want you to think I think the boy did it, Brett. But he might've seen something, heard something. You know that as well as me."

"Right," he said flatly, knowing he should be relieved, angry that he wasn't.

"You want someone else to do it?"

"No. No, I can . . . I'll do it, don't worry."

"Then do it home," Stockton said as he headed back to his office. "No sense making it worse than it is."

He watched the door close silently, stood there in silence until he couldn't stand it anymore. He hurried outside, paused at the top of the steps and stared blindly at the traffic, not feeling the day's heat snake itself around him.

A hand touched his arm gently.

"You feeling all right?" Vicky asked. She was in street clothes, a pants suit practical and cool that somehow managed to disguise her figure. Her hair was tied back; there was perspiration on her brow.

"Fine," he said, smiling wanly and shoving his fingers hard through his hair. "Tell me something," he said then, looking at the street, looking at the houses. "Have you ever wished you were back on the farm?"

"What?"

"Yeah. Don't you wish sometimes you could get the hell out of here and go back to Vermont?"

"Not on your life." She grinned, lifted her right arm, and flexed the biceps. "The only thing I'd get there is more brawn than I'd know what to do with. Thank you, but no. Coming to this place was the best thing I ever did in my life." The grin broadened. "Next, of course, to meeting you."

She winked.

He winked back and hoped she wouldn't see the blush he knew had to be crawling all over his face.

"You off?" she asked then.

He nodded.

"So am I, as of now. You like to join me for a drink? Call it a bracer if you think people will talk."

He laughed and held her arm, half turned and waved with his free hand when a car drove by and the driver honked twice. It was Denise, and she honked again as she turned the corner, a hand arched over the roof and waving.

"I don't think I'd better," he said, and chuckled when he saw the look on Vicky's face. "No, not because of her. I don't want to have . . . I want to be clear-headed when I talk to Les. This heat—one drink and I'll be swinging home through the trees."

"Okay," she said. "Just stop being a stranger from now on, all right? I don't bite, y'know."

His smile was warm. "Okay. That's a promise."

She turned to leave, turned back. "And thanks for holding my hand yesterday. I really appreciate it. It was nice."

He waited until she'd gone before taking the rest of the steps slowly, pulling off his tie and jamming it into his jacket pocket, taking off his jacket and holding it by the collar.

Grateful to the chief for not pressing the issue, he kept his mind a careful blank as he took the long way home, concentrating instead on the rainbows of flowers he saw in the gardens, the late blossoms on some fruit trees that were whitening the lawns, watched a cat stalk a fat robin until he clapped his hands to scare the bird, stuck out his tongue when the cat looked at him and glared.

Marvelous hero of the downtrodden, he thought with a grin, and had a sudden feeling he'd get a call from Denise tonight, casual, and nosey.

And when he reached the house at last, Amy Niles was waiting at the gate. She wore vivid green shorts and a cutoff t-shirt, and the books she held against her chest made her seem almost naked.

He smiled pleasantly, nodded a greeting, and let the smile fade as she backed away from his approach, watching him blankly, her deep-set eyes not shifting, not blinking until he had turned up the walk.

"Mr. Gilman?"

He looked over his shoulder, and stopped.

"Would you tell Les that I tried to call him last night?"

"He wasn't home, Amy," he said, puzzled at the way she kept looking at him. As if he wasn't there. As if he were only a shimmer of heat she was trying to give form.

114

"I know. Would you tell him I called?"

He nodded automatically and she walked away, in and out of the shade, her long legs pale, dark, pale, until a tall hedge intervened and she was gone.

Those legs, however, and the bare midriff, the ribbon of back, were little more than glimpses when he stopped again and cocked his head.

Gone now, unseen, and for the briefest of moments all he heard were her footsteps. Quiet, quick, and muffled. The way they had been in Saturday's fog.

Good god, he thought, and waved away the notion as he climbed heavily to the porch. It was obvious to a blind man she was jealous of whoever went out with Les, but she certainly wasn't crazy enough to follow the son's father as well.

"Nuts," he said as he opened the door. "You're nuts, Gilman. She didn't follow you then, she didn't follow you ever, and she sure as hell didn't kill either of those poor girls."

The house was empty, but there were signs Les had been there—his school jacket had been tossed on the couch, and his books were on the dining room table. The upstairs rooms, though, were empty, and so, when he looked, was the backyard. There was no note.

The car was still in the garage, and he was ashamed that he had checked.

For a while, he stood in the middle of the driveway, trying to make up his mind what to do next. He could wait for Les to show himself, or he could return to the station and face Stockton with the news that the boy was gone. But waiting would kill him; and Stockton only had so much patience to go around. Frustrated, he rolled up his shirtsleeves and considered mowing the lawn, raking the yard, cleaning out the garage, washing the car. And when he was finished stalling, he found himself staring at the fence and thinking of Amy.

He told himself he was crazy, that according to his son and Denise, the girl hadn't been quite the same since her boyfriend had died. On the other hand, it wouldn't be too farfetched for her to latch onto Les because he had helped her; she could hold him, as a lifeline, and feel threatened, unnerved, whenever he saw someone else. Like Evelyn Zayer.

There have been less substantial motives, he thought. A lot less. And for the time being, it was better than the nothing he already had; it was far better than thinking his own boy was a killer.

Forcing down the guilty protests that began instantly to surface, he went inside and checked the telephone book for her address, then changed into jeans and an open-necked shirt. When Les still hadn't arrived by the time he was ready, he told himself Amy was probably having supper with her family—a good time to catch her home, a bad time for questions. So he forced himself to sit down, have a sandwich he barely tasted and a glass of milk he thought sour. A note, then, for Les, apologizing for not being home and asking the boy to forage for his own supper.

Amy wasn't home. No one was.

He stood for a moment at their door, then wandered over to Chancellor Avenue, trying to decide where best to find her, or get hold of Les. He had started for the luncheonette when he saw her heading for Mainland Road.

An impulse to call out was denied, and he followed instead, hands loose in his pockets. He was strolling, nothing more, as the last of the sun glared hard in his eyes and the heat broke drops of perspiration along the line of his hair. This was the way she'd gone when he'd seen her with Les, and he wondered if the field, the deserted Armstrong farm, was a meeting place for kids. He'd heard no word of it, believing that the local lovers' lanes were confined to the valley on the other side of the tracks.

She paused at the corner before crossing over,

down into the drainage ditch, up through the brambles.

A truck hurtled by, and he turned away from the blast of hot air that made his cheeks feel dry and cracked.

Dumb, he thought, and sprinted over, scrambling up the slope, squinting as the light shot red into his eyes, obscuring everything but the points of thorns quivering near his face. He waited, catching his breath, then slipped sideways along the hedge until he found a gap he could push through.

A pale curling mist was lifting from the field, drifting out of the trees north and south of him to wind through the weeds. He stretched his neck, rubbed his shoulders, picked up a stick and started walking. Westward, but not directly. Peering down into the dead high grass, switching aside browning stalks, watching a pair of grasshoppers whirr like cracked paper away from his shoes.

Out for a stroll.

Shading his eyes against the sun now caged behind the trees, the air difficult to breathe, his chest growing tight, locusts in the trees buzzing louder than the traffic. Stumbling over a hidden burrow that nearly turned his ankle. Kicking a branch to one side and ducking away from a swarm of spinning gnats he snorted from his nostrils, scratched out of his ears. Watching burrs cling to his legs and wobble with his motion.

Then he heard his name—a whisper, a calling—and she was standing by the near edge of the orchard, the dead and burned trees sharp and more lifeless as the day shaded faintly gold.

She smiled shyly when he reached her, still switching the weeds, once in a while taking the stick lightly to his leg. "Are you following me again, Mr. Gilman?"

He laughed. "No. I have been looking for you, though."

She frowned briefly. "Why?"

He looked behind her, at the few blades of green that poked through the hardened ash, at the gnarled and blackened branches, at the green fields beyond, where a flock of sparrows rose and settled, rose again and circled. It was a dismal place, and he couldn't help shaking as if he were cold, couldn't help wondering why anyone would want to even look at this place.

"Good lord, Amy," he said, still smiling, "do you come out here a lot?"

"Sometimes."

"It's like a graveyard, for Pete's sake. Aren't there better places to go, prettier ones?"

She reached behind her and pulled at a charred twig. "Mike was here. We had . . . a bunch of us had a picnic, Mr. Gilman, and he wanted me to marry him."

He kept his silence; he tossed the stick away.

She knelt and used her twig to poke at the ground, at an anthill that seemed as dead as the orchard. Her free hand slapped at her hair to drive off a fly. "I used to think, you know, about knights and things? Shining armor and all that." A look up. "Is that silly?"

"No," he said honestly. "Not at all."

"Miss Quarell doesn't think so, either. She says that as long as there are people like me, there's hope for the world." Her laugh was quick, light, and scattered by the wind. "I wanted, when I was a little girl, to put my head in a unicorn's lap, or have a prince climb a tower and save me, or have some movie star come up and take me away in his limousine." Another laugh, cold and without mirth. "Miss Quarell says I have to be careful what I dream."

"And what do your parents say?"

She stood, took a deep breath, and lifted her arms languidly over her head, and he couldn't avoid looking at the flat of her tanned stomach, the lower slopes of her small breasts gleaming as if oiled.

"Get good grades, graduate, and get a good job."

"Not bad advice, Amy," he said uneasily, when she took a step toward him and he didn't back away. "Practical."

As close as the length of a finger, she looked into his eyes and he dared not look away. A hand pushed away a trailing lock of her hair, and her lips began to twist into a one-sided smile. "He's afraid of you, you know."

"Who?" he said, his voice harsh and strained.

Closer, and he could feel her naked stomach push gently against his belt.

"Leslie, who else? He thinks you're going to arrest him because you think he's a killer." She giggled, and her tongue brushed pink across her lips. "He wants to run away, Mr. Gilman. And he wants me to go with him."

He grabbed her waist angrily to shove her aside; she clapped her palms to his cheeks, pulled his face down, and kissed him hard, thrust her hips into his before twisting away.

"He's not yours anymore," she said, starting to run. "He isn't. He's mine."

Too surprised to move, too confused to think, he watched as she dashed across the open ground, turning once to grin before she vanished through the hedge.

"God Almighty." He wiped a hand over his mouth, over his eyes. "Good God Almighty."

He wondered then how often Denise had spoken with the girl, if she had ever followed Amy out here as he had done; he wondered if she suspected what the girl had become.

Les, he thought suddenly; Christ, he had to get to Les and find out what was going on. But the step he took faltered when he tasted the girl's mouth on his, her cool skin in his hands.

God, what the hell's the matter with you? he told himself.

A cigarette in his hand, the match lit, gone, tossed over his shoulder.

He didn't know.

Since this case had begun he'd been walking around as if in a daze. Normal procedures seemed to blossom into major obstacles, and under ordinary circumstances he sure as hell wouldn't have followed a young woman all the way out here just to ask her a couple of questions. He would have waited at the house. He would have gone to the college and waited for her there. He would have done a hundred other things. But he hadn't.

And now, abruptly, he was feeling terribly alone. As though everyone he cared for was drawing slowly away.

A glance down at his shadow, spiked and gored by the grass and the weeds. It was harder to see as the mist thickened and rose, and he shook his head

quickly, looked at his cigarette and realized it had
burnt down to the filter, and he was sure he hadn't
taken more than one puff. The ash still there was
cold.

"Christ," he whispered, and heard the footsteps
behind him.

He turned slowly, tense in case he had to react,
ready with a smile in case it was only someone
just out for a walk.

No one was there.

His head tilted slightly to one side, his ears
strained, his eyes narrowed in the dusk suddenly
upon him.

No one was there.

Mist into patchy fog as if something was burning deep beneath the surface.

A slow and steady walk, light, quiet.

And finally, back in the shadows of the orchard's far side, a hint of something white moving
around the boles.

He stepped to his right for a clearer view, cran-
ing now, one hand slapping his leg nervously.

"Hey!"

Tall and white and long, without definite form
yet anything but spectral as he took a step forward,
checked himself, and stepped hastily back when a
gust of wind spun ash in a dervish, when he

realized that whatever was back there was pacing and watching.

"Hey, who are you? This is the police! What are you doing out here?"

He almost giggled. His voice quavered, authority shredded, and the command on the face of it was ludicrous and weak. He started toward the figure, stopped at the orchard's edge and waited for another gust to pass, listening as it rattled through the trees and hissed like sand through the field.

And when it was over, he didn't want to go in.

Moving farther to his right, he thought to circle the fire-spot and come at the watcher from behind. Tripping over a hillock and nearly landing on his shoulder. Slapping impatiently at the gnats that returned to bedevil him, dancing black and swift in front of his eyes no matter which way he looked. Picking up another stick and using it to knock away weeds whose heads were like dried wheat, branches that would not give, the dark that increased as the sun dropped and died. Reaching the last of the apple trees and skirting them, a headache building behind his forehead as he stared even harder to keep the white shape in sight.

Pacing, watching, quietly and soft.

Telling himself it was only a gag, that he was the butt of a prank, and before he went much farther some of Les's friends would throw off a thin sheet and laugh at his nervousness, his gullibility, and ask him snidely if Amy Niles was his girl.

He stopped.

A slither of grey ash rounded the toe of his left foot.

His right hand slashed the stick through the air, a cat's tail expending anger, testing fear.

Pacing, in the mist, and footsteps hard and hollow.

He blinked rapidly and swallowed, demanding to know what in god's name had gotten into him? If it was a joke, what the hell was he doing playing along, walking right into it like some kind of fool?

He turned sharply and stalked away, hurriedly when he reached the field again, almost running when he was less than a hundred yards from the road. He hoped they were watching. He hoped they saw how he didn't much care for their stupid jokes, their infantile notions of what was supposed to be funny. He hoped that whatever it was back there . . . *who*ever it was, he told himself angrily. Whoever, not whatever. Because it's only kids in a sheet and you know it, you jackass, you know what they want and you won't let them have it.

He plunged through the hedge without looking

for a gap, grunting at the thorns that tore at his shirt, scratched his hands, and drew blood; across the road and into town as the streetlamps buzzed on and the pavement writhed with shadows.

Scared, he thought in amazement; Jesus, I'm scared.

He rejected the notion with a disdainful snort, saw shadows, heard footsteps, and felt the fear again.

This time he didn't fight it—he ran, knowing he had to talk to Les, to tell him what Amy had done there in the field, to try to stop him from running away, from ruining his life. From deserting his father.

Heedless of his appearance, knowing he must look like someone fresh from a beating, he ran until he fell against the fence around his yard, panting, wrinkling his nose at the sweat that poured from his hair, rolling his shoulders against the sweat that turned his shirt flat cold. He gasped and leaned back, hands propping him up on either side, gulping the night air and feeling his heart build pressure in his chest. His legs buckled, but he didn't fall. His head throbbed at the temples, but he didn't close his eyes.

"Damn," he said. "Jesus, *damn*."

He waited until he was sure he wouldn't faint, then staggered up the walk and dropped onto the porch. Waited a minute more and almost fell through the door, calling for his son and hearing only the silence, seeing only the outlines of furniture in the feeble light from the street.

"Les," he called as he hauled himself up the stairs, stripping off his shirt, kicking off his shoes. "Les, goddamnit, don't you do this to me!"

The hall was empty, Les's bedroom, his own.

Swiftly, he changed into dry clothes and called Denise, without luck, immediately called Vicky and explained that it looked like his boy had gotten scared and had run away—and he nearly broke into grateful tears when she told him to hold on, she was already in her car and cruising the streets, don't worry, love, we'll find him before he does anything stupid, we'll find him, don't worry, just calm down and go looking yourself when you can.

At the front door he paused, hand on the knob. She had called him "love." He smiled. And the smile faded when he shook his head violently, not needing that now, needing only his son.

He stepped out, car keys in hand, and called Les again when he saw someone on the walk.

"No, sir," Lonrow said, puzzled. "It's me."

Oh, god, please no.

"What is it, Nick? Is it Les?"

Lonrow shook his head. "The Chief sent me for you, sir. She's in the park."

He grabbed a post and leaned against it. "Who?" he said wearily.

"Amy Niles," the man answered. "Someone saw her and your . . . saw her and Les go into the park about an hour ago." He turned away, stared at the elm. "She's dead. Your son's gone."

The park's high iron fence formed a slatted black wall when the gates closed behind him. There were a dozen or more of the curious on the street, and he could hear them talking, whispering, as he followed Lonrow quickly up a winding tarmac path, then through a break in thick laurel on his right. Directly ahead, across a wide stretch of grass, a tall stand of pine stood between him and the pond; on his left was open ground, which eventually rose to a low hill, whose face had been cleared and whose crown was black with low brush and trees. Midway to the rise was an unofficial ballfield, and he could see several men moving about, stick figures dancing jerkily against blaring flashbulbs and four high-intensity spotlights fixed on ten-foot tripods placed at each of the bases.

The fog reached for the lights, blurred the men's outlines, and again he was reminded of something burning underground.

No one looked up as he approached; they only backed away to let him see.

There was a low cordon of rope enclosing most of the infield; there was no one inside except Amy Niles.

She was lying on an irregular bare patch of earth used for the pitcher's mound: on her back, t-shirt only half covering her breasts, brown hair bleached to dull grey by the strength of the artificial light. Her arms were flung out and back, one leg was tucked up, one ankle bloodied, nothing on her face but a coating of fine dust, and by the look of the ground around her, she had been tossed around in a manic frenzy, or had been fighting whoever had killed her.

His legs moved, though he didn't want them to; his hands relaxed, though he wanted someone to hit. When he reached her, he knelt, closed his eyes, touched her arm and felt the last of her warmth seep into the ground.

"Tell me," he whispered, and Lonrow was there.

"A lady—she's back there with Chief Stockton—she said she was coming home from shopping when she saw Les and Amy run in here. They were laughing, horsing around; the woman said she didn't hear any shouting or anything. She figured they were just kids, y'know?"

There was too much blood on her chest, but not enough to hide the hole.

"Who found her?"

"The night patrol." Lonrow cleared his throat and coughed harshly. "They were on routine through the park and thought they saw something out here. So they looked and . . . and they found her. The woman, the one who saw them come in, she lives across the street. When she saw the cars, she came out."

Brett rose abruptly, and the young man nearly stumbled as he got out of the way. "Keep everyone out of here but me," he was told, and didn't have time to nod before Brett was heading across the infield, watching where he put his feet before he stepped over the rope.

Stockton was still in uniform, and he took Brett's arm, led him into the shadows and swore so viciously, so suddenly, Brett couldn't help gaping. "I *hate* this sonofabitching job," he said then. "I *hate* kids dying." Brett could barely see his face, and what he did see he didn't like. "You'll have to bring the boy in, son. He's gotta tell us what he knows."

Brett swung between hatred and anguish, chewing hard on his lips until he tasted salt and blood. "You think . . . you think now he did it?"

"Just bring him in, Brett. Do what you have to do out here, then get him and bring him to me. I'll take it from there."

*   *   *

He was left alone once the body had been taken. In the dead harsh white he scoured the field, sectioning it with his mind's eye and crawling over it on his knees. The hot lights kept the fog from interfering, building a white wall, killing the stars, muffling the sounds of the Station and magnifying his panting, the scrape of his knees on the dirt, the occasional grunt when he thought he'd found something and found it was nothing at all.

Until he saw the prints.

They were in a worn trough that served as a baseline, and he remembered seeing them before, behind the theater, under the trees.

This time they were clearer, and he circled them carefully, scowling because he didn't know what they were, exasperated because he knew what they weren't—no animal in the village ever had paws or hooves like these.

He sighed, and unexpectedly yawned, rubbed his eyes fiercely, swallowed and realized his throat was filled with dust. As he walked to loosen his legs, drive the tension from his back, he knew there was little more he could do now, at least not until he had cleared his head, had something to drink, and had had a chance to find Les and talk.

The patrolman on guard at the gate nodded when Brett told him to keep the place locked until he returned, and he felt the man watching him keenly as he started for home. He knew what the man was thinking—a cop with a son for a killer, and redemption was something that happened only in the movies.

Les was in the living room when he came in the door.

"Jesus, Dad," he said, standing quickly, his face pinched with worry. "Jesus, what am I gonna do?"

Brett sagged against the door and waved a weary hand. "Where were you?" he asked. "Where the hell have you been?"

"Out."

"No shit," he snapped. "I've been looking for you all goddamned day!" He raised his head and glared. "Stockton wants me to bring you in. To talk," he added hastily. "There aren't any charges; you don't have to worry."

Les laughed, but there was no humor in his smile. "Oh, right, Dad, sure. No charges. But let's not forget that Les was with each of those girls before they died, okay? And I suppose you know that Amy and I went for a walk in the park, too. I know she talked to you. She told me." And his arm lashed out at Brett's chair, knocking it several inches to one side.

Brett nodded, wanting to go over there and put his arms around the boy, comfort him, say something that would banish the fear. But he couldn't move. Not now. Now he was a cop, and now he was a father, and now he wished to hell Stockton wasn't so goddamned understanding.

"So now what?" Les said dully.

"Now . . . now you tell me how you knew about this. The radio? Someone call? What?"

"Denise," the boy said.

Brett stared at him stupidly. "Denise?"

"Right. That's where I've been since school practically. Jesus, didn't you know any of that?" He laughed again, and sniffed as if he were trying not to cry. "*She* talks to me, Dad. *She* had the time. *She's* the one who told me I ought to think about moving out."

"She . . . what?"

Les started for the kitchen, changed his mind, and stopped in front of him. "Yeah, right. I'm eighteen, remember? It's legal. And I sure don't get much sympathy around here."

Brett covered his face, dropped his hands. "That's crazy, boy. This isn't the time to talk about it, but you aren't moving out. Certainly not now."

"Why? Because you think I killed my friends?"

Brett raised a hand to slap him and Les grabbed the wrist to force it back down. "You can't hold me anymore, Dad. You can't. You don't let me breathe, I have to check in and check out like I was some kind of—''

Brett yanked his hand free and slammed its heel against the boy's shoulder, knocking him back to arm's distance. ''I told you this wasn't the time for that. You don't seem to realize, boy, what the hell's happening.'' He stopped to take a breath, take another. ''Now listen to me and no arguments. Get your coat. You're coming with me so we can straighten it all out. Now. Before it gets any worse.''

''The hell I am. I'll go by myself.''

He was too shaken to resist when Les moved him out of the way and opened the door; he was too torn between rage and weeping to prevent him from running down the walk, vaulting the gate, and disappearing into the dark. And when he finally stopped trembling, finally dispelled the sensation he was suffocating in a coffin, he grabbed up the telephone and dialed Denise's number.

Who the hell did she think she was, handing out advice like that, especially to his son? She knew full well the kind of trouble the boy was facing. What she was doing didn't make any sense.

''Hello?''

And she had told Amy that practical was out and dreaming was all right.

''Hello?''

"Denise," he said, his voice hollow.

Jesus, it was as if she actually wanted him—

"Oh, Brett, thank god! I was so worried about you. I heard about poor Amy and I couldn't imagine—"

He hung up.

He stared at the receiver, heard her voice, heard echoes of other words and finally cornered them, listened to them, and realized what they'd been doing.

He was being isolated.

He was being eased into a room with no doors, no windows, and only she had the means to get him out again.

Dream, she had told Amy; dream, and it'll be yours.

With a directionless oath he raced for the door, flung it open, and charged down the walk. The gate latch jammed, and he yanked the whole thing off its hinges, swung left and ran, for the first few seconds paying no heed to a car that sped after him, slowed, and began blaring its horn to stop him. When he did turn, he saw Victoria, and when she braked, he skirted the hood without slowing and jumped in beside her.

"I saw Les," she told him as he waved her to drive on. "He was running, and I couldn't get him to stop. Brett, what's—"

"Later," he said. "We'll get him later and straighten it all out. Right now, go to the park. There's something there I need you to see. I need your help."

She kept glancing at him, but he refused to meet her gaze, staring instead at the street ahead, at the clouds of fog in the trees, at the image of Amy in the orchard, and Amy on the ground.

The patrolman had the gates open as Vicky skidded to a halt at the curb, and said nothing when they ran inside, following the path to the field, slowing, and stopping.

The lights were still on.

He took her hand and brought her to the place where Amy had fallen, tersely explaining what he had seen, then took her over to show her the prints. She said nothing as she hunkered down beside them, brushing her hair back over her shoulders, tilting her head from one side to the other, and freezing when they heard someone moving toward them out there, beyond the white wall the fog formed with the light.

"What are they?" he asked quietly, tapping her shoulder to bring her to her feet.

The wall of white sparkled like mica when a breeze shifted the mist.

"Like a horse," she whispered, "only they're not quite right."

"A horse?"

She nodded, and looked down again.

"What's wrong with them? Too small?" He looked around and took her arm.

"No. Just . . . not right."

One of the lights snapped out and there was black behind them.

Slowly, listening to the footsteps, steady and quiet, he pulled her with him as he backed away, shaking his head when she questioned him with a look, damning whatever had made him leave his gun at the house.

A second light flared to blind them, and died a moment later, spraying sparks to the grass and hissing at the fog. Their shadows crossed on the ground, aiming for the trees.

"Brett," she whispered.

The third light, and the fourth, and he was frozen by the dark, squinting as he waited for his night vision to work, holding her arm tighter, waving his free hand in front of him as if to hold back the footsteps that sounded now like drums.

And when he saw it, saw the moon over the trees and the greylight it cast, he stopped and released her and waited for Denise.

He had no idea what she had used for a weapon, but he thought now he knew why—to drive Les away. They were too close, too well knit by the death of their family, and Brett wouldn't let the boy go. The killings had brought pressures on them both, making him cling even harder and aggravating Les's drive for independence. Using Amy, alive, and using Amy, dead. Using his guilt, and his grief. Forcing him to remember Grace and his daughter, asking all those questions to prove he couldn't make it alone, not anymore, not without her.

He turned to Vicky with a bitter smile, to tell her what he knew, and felt the air leave his lungs as if he'd been punched. She was gone, and he could barely see her making her way toward the low hill, crouching, gun in hand, heading for a dark figure midway up toward the trees.

He called out and started to run.

She whirled and gestured angrily, turned again, and Denise had moved to the right, out of the shadows and into the light.

"Stop! Vicky, Jesus, stop!" he screamed, but he misjudged the way the park rose, and he stumbled, fell, scrambled on hands and knees until he could stand again. Walking now, slowly, finding his breath as he kept Victoria on his left, himself the point of the triangle.

Then Denise laughed in delight as the moon brightened, and he saw her as she wanted to be seen—young, and lovely, her eyes glinting silver and her teeth gleaming white and the flow of her figure something to hold. But the laugh held no warmth, and the silver was cold, and the gleam turned her mouth to a beast's, filled with fangs.

When he stopped, she fell silent, and shook her head with a rueful smile.

"You never dreamed, you know," she told him, quietly though he could hear her, sweetly though he tasted bile. "You were always the cop with imagination, but you never dreamed about being rescued, you never wished for a gallant knight to save you from the dragon."

Oh, god, he thought; oh, god, she's insane.

"I never had to," he answered gently, taking one step toward her and stopping when she frowned, looking over to Victoria, who still held the gun. "I always had what I wanted. I didn't have to pretend."

She backed away, and the shadow of a broken pine split her neatly in half. "No," she said. "You never did, you know. You never really had Grace, and you never really had Les, and unless you have me, Brett, you won't even have you."

He didn't dare look, but he hoped Vicky wasn't listening and was circling around behind. Though Denise didn't appear to have a weapon, he remembered the bodies and couldn't risk taking her on himself.

"Denise," he said sadly, "I'm not your knight."

She giggled and covered her mouth with one hand.

A glance behind him, to the ballfield, and all he saw was the fog laying down a rolling grey blanket.

"Denise."

She raised an eyebrow.

"Denise, look, everything you've said to me now, you told Amy, remember? The knights and the movie stars. But god, there aren't any knights left, and there are no movie stars here, and, Jesus, didn't you tell her to be careful what she dreamed?"

The shadowed head nodded, and the shadowvoice said, "I know, and I meant it." And the shadowvoice hardened. "You were so damned worried about yourself, afraid that you'd be alone, that you scared yourself out of living, Brett. You scared yourself to death."

"Denise—"

A hand lifted, a finger pointed, and Brett felt the cold, and the fog, and night.

"Dreams," she said, "can be very real, you know. They can be as real as you want them, when you want them, when you want someone to love."

Then Victoria screamed and fired twice. He spun around to yell, and dropped to his knees when Denise didn't fall and Vicky fired twice again and he saw the night shimmer at the top of the hill.

Rising like a nightflower against the full of the moon, lifting slowly to a grey silhouette that raised its head high, that held its forelegs still, that turned one red eye to the park spread below it and listened for the sound that would signal its charge.

Listened, and waited, and as the moon rose higher above the knoll where it stood, it just as slowly lowered itself back to the ground. Its mane was dark and curling in the wind, its tail the same and bannered behind it, though the wind that moved them never touched the grass, never stirred the trees, never whispered to the creatures that burrowed deeper underground.

A leg lifted and struck the earth softly, and there was a cascade of sparks, a crimson plume of fire, and it backed away quickly and struck fire again.

Waiting. Always patient.

Against the dark-crater moon like a daemon in white amber.

"*I* did it," she whispered as Brett crawled toward Vicky, his eye on the creature that watched him, and waited.

It was a trick, but it cast a shadow, and the

grass still smoldered where it had raised crimson fire.

"*I* dreamed," she said with a laugh as she came around behind him, neither stopping nor helping, only following in his wake.

Then it lifted its head again, and he saw the spiraled horn.

"I dreamed and dreamed so goddamned hard," was the whisper out of the dark, out of the fog, "that it came just like it should have, and it put its head in my lap."

He reached Victoria and lay a hand on her chest, felt the struggling heartbeat and took the gun, then saw the blood matting her hair, heard the creature stirring, saw its shadow move toward him.

"Didn't you ever wonder," Denise said, kneeling just out of reach, "why all the pictures, all those tapestries, show men hunting them with weapons, why dogs had to be used if they were so gentle? Didn't you ever wonder what the horn was for?"

A trick, he thought; a trick, it's a trick.

"They're not, you know. They're not gentle at all."

She hit his shoulder with a heavy stone, and he whirled, the gun up and aimed shaking at her breast.

She smiled in the moonlight and glanced up the hill.

Victoria groaned and stirred.

"You'll have to choose, Brett."

Victoria sat up, touched her head gingerly, and gasped when her hand came away running with blood.

"Denise, this is—"

"Choose now, Brett," she said calmly. "But think before you do. If you shoot me, that woman will leave you. Sooner or later, she'll leave because you'll remind her of what happened tonight, and she's not strong enough to live with it. She's not strong at all." The smile softened, and filled with love. "You'll be alone, Brett, all alone. No matter what happens, Les will be gone."

He couldn't move, he couldn't think; he heard Victoria whimpering and the creature pawing the ground, heard Denise still whispering and the blood roaring in his ears, heard Les damning him for loving too well.

"I can make you forget," was the promise he heard. "And I can make it go away."

He shook his head.

Victoria cried.

"And if you don't choose me—"

Her scream, then, was the last thing he heard before he squeezed the trigger and watched her flail to the ground; the last thing he saw before he spun on his knees and knew she was wrong.

Victoria was standing by the creature's lowered head, stroking its mane, whispering fondly in its ear. Then she looked down at him and smiled, and stroked the length of its horn.

"I have dreams, too," she said. "I have dreams, too."

And he saw her in the moonlight, tall and sweet and fair, waiting for his answer on a bed of crimson fire.

Part Three

The Last and Dreadful Hour

Summer, in Oxrun, died in a storm.

The afternoon had been warm for the last day of September, but the leaves had already started to turn, the ducks on the pond already gone in a twilight flight that called out to the village and brought on the dark. No one wore a coat, but sweaters were taken out to be aired in the yard, gloves were found in drawers and closets, and windows were checked for betrayals of draughts. Fur thickened, pavement hardened, boilers and furnaces practiced their steam.

It was warm for the last day of September, but those leaving work just after five saw the clouds on the horizon, moving toward the valley east of the tracks: white, and puffed, and sharp-edged against the blue. And the same drifting over the hills south and north, like desert clouds building their frozen billowing smoke: white, and puffed, and sharp-edged against the blue. And a single massive cloud that crawled out of the west, its shadow creeping across the fields like a shade drawn against the sun: grey, and boiling, and smothering the blue.

The wind began to blow just after six, in no particular direction as the clouds merged at their rims, forming a funnel above the village that looked up to the blue shrinking to the size of a platter, a coin, an eye that closed tightly when all the clouds turned to black.

Leaves ran in gutters, paper slapped against doors, dust in dark tornadoes bounced across the grass to explode against walls; hats were blown off, faces turned away, and on Fox Road near the cemetery a loose, flapping shutter chipped its paint against clapboard until a hinge snapped, a nail loosened, and it spun to the ground. The flag over the high school entrance began to shred. A line of wash on Barlow Street tore loose and was snagged on the branches of a dying pine. The sidewalk displays in front of Buller's Market were carted inside by clerks, who swore angrily when their aprons whipped their legs and their hair whipped their eyes. Neon flickered on, street lamps cast shadows, the amber light at Mainland Road and the Pike jerked and swayed, danced and spun, until it sputtered, brightened, and winked out without a sound.

The rain began just after seven.

The film in the Regency started just at seven-thirty.

The lights dimmed once, just after eight.

And summer, in Oxrun Station, died in a storm.

The Regency Theater was less than two years new, and had been constructed old-fashioned because the owner was tired of tiny figures on tiny screens pretending to be much larger than they were.

The exterior was deliberately houselike, red brick and white trim, no marquee and no posters, and the ticket booth was flush with the glass doors that flanked it. There were windows as well, white-curtained, with white tasseled shades pulled midway down the sash, and more than one visitor looked in to see what the living room was like.

What they saw was darkly polished black oak wainscoting topped with pearl-and-silver flocked paper, ivy and leaves and just a suggestion of trees; the thick wall-to-wall carpet was Oriental, floral, its background a royal blue and vacuumed

three times a night; and along the back wall, between the entrances to the auditorium, were thickly
upholstered high-backed couches, Queen Anne
chairs, and silver ashtray stands. To the left and
right in the corners were red-carpeted staircases
leading to the balcony, and in shallow alcoves
beside each a small concession stand.

But the Regency's pride was the theater itself.

The screen was a monster that tipped your head
back when you sat in the front row, the ceiling
slightly domed and painted in constellations that
glowed for a moment when the houselights went
down; the walls on the sides were draped in dark
red velvet, the seats upholstered and wide; and
there was a steep-angled balcony that extended ten
rows over the main floor. A uniformed usher with
a hooded flashlight guided the way to patrons'
places; there were Saturday matinees that showed
nothing but old horror films, five cartoons, and a
trailer, and the manager could usually be found
standing stiffly at the back, unafraid to eject the
rowdy and keep the popcorn in its boxes.

And as the last show ended, the credits still
running and the lights slowly brightening in their
bronze brackets on the walls, the electricity failed
and the building went dark.

"Oh, wonderful," Ellery muttered and slumped
back in his seat, glaring at the dark as if he could

bring the lights back simply by threatening them with damnation. It was, without question, the only possible end to an already miserable day, and he wasn't surprised when the manager's voice soon came over the sound system and apologized for the inconvenience, asking the customers still remaining to please stay where they were until the staff came around with lights to guide them out.

Why the hell not, he thought; if I go home, the place will have probably been struck by lightning.

He heard without listening to the voices drifting around him—only a few, if he was right, and someone laughing giddily in the balcony.

A minute passed, too long for his comfort, and a man to his far left began a strident complaint, arguing with someone, evidently his wife. He couldn't see who it was, couldn't see anyone at all, and the more he strained, the closer he came to giving himself a headache. The people in the balcony—there couldn't have been more than two— laughed even louder, and the noise echoed in the huge auditorium, merging, distorting, and soon after, he felt the first tear of perspiration grow cold on his brow.

"Easy, El," he whispered, and pulled his rain-coat close to his chest. "Take it easy. It won't last."

But the perspiration was there, and the muffled

thunder above, the sounds of things—people! —moving without waiting for someone to help them.

"Easy," he said, but he couldn't help the acid that started to build in his stomach.

He didn't like the dark.

It was stupid, and it was silly, and most certainly childish. But no matter how often he told himself at home that he could easily close the bedroom drapes and keep out the streetlight and moonlight without any problem, he didn't. The shadows were better than no shadows at all, and a lamp burned in the living room until he came down for breakfast.

Another minute, and he shook out his raincoat, touched his throat, and stood, grabbing for the seat in front and sidling to his left until he reached the aisle, proud he hadn't sliced open his shin on the chairs' curved metal legs. The manager once again assured them they would soon be able to see, but he couldn't wait. He wanted to get out. He wanted to see something, even if it were only shadows against a lighter dark.

Then the lobby doors swung open and shimmering white swept down the aisle. There was good-humored applause, suddenly excited chatter, and soon he was able to distinguish black figures easing out of the rows, the complaining man now laughing along with those still upstairs.

He paused for a moment, struggling into his raincoat and scolding himself for almost losing control. But it was, he thought, symptomatic of the way things had been going these past few days—as if he had been latched onto by a gremlin determined to make him look like a fool.

Nice, he thought then; good sane thinking, El. Keep it up, they'll have you safely locked away before you can sneeze.

His arm caught in a sleeve where the lining was frayed. He closed his eyes, took a breath, and rammed it through, smiling when he felt the worn threads tear at the wrist.

And as he watched the others file toward the lobby, he frowned in the realization he had been practically alone for the entire show. Not that it was surprising. The storm had renewed itself vigorously just after he'd decided that sitting home alone wasn't going to do his depression any good. The bars were out because he wasn't much of a drinker, there was no one he could call for a shoulder to use, and going back to the botch he had made of his day's work would only depress him further. So he came to a movie. And even now he'd be hard-pressed to explain what it had been about.

A figure partially blocked the glow at the head of his aisle, large and formless, hands on its wide hips as it kicked doorstops into place. Callum Davidson, the manager, shepherding his people out of the abyss. Ellery sighed and started up, the dim light slowing him so he wouldn't trip on a chair leg or stumble over his own feet. Davidson turned and left; another figure took his place, one with a flashlight that aimed straight into his eyes. He turned his head, raised a hand, and the usher apologized, lowered the beam to the floor, and waited.

At the back row, Ellery smoothed his coat's lapels and turned around, to see the screen framed in black; it looked as if it were glowing.

"Weird, huh?" the usher said, stabbing his flashlight at the stage. "Happens all the time. Absorbs the light or something, Mr. Davidson says, and makes it look like some kind of monster TV screen."

"Seth," Ellery said to the young man sourly, "Mr. Davidson has a lousy imagination."

The usher shrugged.

Easy, Ellery told himself; it isn't the kid's fault.

He turned to apologize, and lifted his head when he heard what he thought was someone falling, and falling hard. Seth heard it, too, and after exchanging alarmed glances, they stepped back down the aisle, trying to see past the flashlight's reach, listening for a moan or a crying or someone swearing as he got back to his feet. But the only sounds were the distant rumble of thunder and the muffled chatter of the people in the lobby.

"I heard it," he said when they reached the first row, the screen looming behind him. "I know I did."

Seth shifted the light from one hand to the other and rubbed his chest nervously. "I know. Me, too. Here," and they moved to the other aisle and started back up, slowly, then more rapidly as they approached the last seats and Ellery had about decided they had made a mistake.

They found him in the corner, slumped on the floor.

"Oh, Jesus," the usher said as Ellery squeezed into the row, his shadow blotting out the fallen man until Seth ran around the back wall and poked the light through the short drapes that blocked the lobby's glow from the theater. The brass rings that held the velvet on its rod rattled too much like bones, and Ellery knelt quickly, reached out a hand and pulled it back.

"You'd better get Callum," he said, and was handed the long silver cylinder.

The man was old without an age, his hair sparse and white, his face lightly tinged as if he had jaundice. His coat was worn, and when Ellery pulled back a lapel, he saw a suit underneath, a white shirt, a black knitted tie pulled away from the collar. The eyes were closed, but a touch of his hand to the man's boney chest and the side of his scrawny neck proved a heartbeat, which made him sigh and lean back, wipe a hand over his forehead and dry it on his thigh.

Davidson arrived in a hurry and leaned over the wall, staring as Ellery played the flashlight along the old man's body.

"Is he dead?"

"No."

"What the hell happened?"

"I guess he tripped."

"Wonderful."

"God, you think maybe he had a heart attack or something?" Seth whispered, a suggestion Ellery didn't want to hear and the manager snorted at.

"You know who he is, El?"

He shook his head. "Never saw him before."

"Is there something wrong?" a voice asked, and he looked to the end of the row, at a young woman peering anxiously through the gloom.

"Toni?" he said.

She took a step in. "Mr. Phillips? Mr. Phillips, are you okay?"

"It's not me, thank god," he answered, stood, and pointed at the old man.

"Let me take a look."

He looked to Davidson and shrugged *why not?*, pressing as best he could against the seatback behind him while she squeezed past. She was wearing a white T-shirt and washed-out jeans, and it was all he could do to resist patting her rump as she passed. When she knelt down, he explained softly to Callum that she was a student at Hawksted College, her father a doctor and she studying to be the same. She used to come often to the bookshop, and there were times, more than several, when he wished he were ten years younger.

"He's knocked his head pretty good," she said without looking up. "There's a nasty bruise here."

"Heart attack?" Callum asked.

"No, I doubt it. But I think you'd better get a doctor here just in case."

"Toni," Ellery said softly, "we can't leave him there on the floor."

"It's okay to move him, if that's what you're worried about," she answered. "Just be careful of his head, okay?" Then she straightened, rubbed a hand over the back of her neck, and waved him out to the aisle. He grinned and did as he was told, thanked her when she joined him, took her arm and pulled her down a pace while Davidson and

Seth moved to carry the old man to the manager's office.

"I haven't seen you for a while," he said quietly, feeling the dark on his back, watching the two men swaying away with their burden.

She looked up at him and, after a long moment's study, smiled sadly. His hand was taken in hers, and he felt the cold there in her long, soft fingers, as he felt a cold he hadn't noticed before filling the auditorium, seeping through the walls from the storm outside. It made him shiver and hunch his shoulders, and she tightened her grip briefly before letting him go.

"I've been around," she whispered.

"Busy with the new semester?" and let her pull him slowly up the aisle toward the light.

She shook her head. "I didn't go back."

"What? No kidding. Well, why not, Toni? I thought you were doing so well."

She stopped and faced him, eyes hidden in shadow, features blurred. "Things are different, Mr. Phillips," she said, in a quiet voice, a low voice.

He wasn't sure what to say, didn't know what she meant and called himself a damned fool for just standing there and smiling.

Then she tilted her head to one side, her lips

slightly parted, colorless, and dry. "Have you ever been to the orchard, Mr. Phillips?"

"Huh? What are you . . . what orchard?"

"There's an orchard. On the other side of Mainland Road, on the old Armstrong farm. Some of it's dead, some of it's not."

He shifted to step around her, to move up the aisle back to the others. He hadn't the slightest idea what the hell she was talking about, but he was afraid she had changed too much for him to know her.

"It's really nice there," she said still whispering, taking a sidestep to block him. "I had a picnic there once."

"Picnics are good things," he told her, wincing at how inane he must sound. "I used to go on them myself when I was younger." Thinking: She's on something, that's why she's not in school anymore. What a hell of a thing to happen to such a nice kid. A hell of a thing. "But I have to admit I've never—"

"It's cold there," she said. "Really cold."

He looked over her shoulder for someone to help him, and unconsciously pulled his raincoat closed against the chill that still worked the theater.

"Toni, look, why don't we—"

"Be careful," she whispered then. "I wasn't

159

kidding before. Things are different now, Mr. Phillips. Things aren't ever going to be the same.''

And before he could move away, she leaned against him and kissed his cheek, released his hand, and ran away.

Leaving him in the flickering twilight of the auditorium, one finger touching the cold mark of her lips while thunder whispered in the black above his head.

Seconds later, realizing he had been left alone, he rushed into the lobby, paused to let his eyes adjust to the light, then turned left and stepped into Davidson's small, cluttered office beside the concession stand. Seth was waiting glumly by the door. The old man was lying on a leather couch, his overcoat for a blanket.

''Did you call the police, a doctor?'' he asked.

Davidson shook his head and pointed to his desk. ''Phone's out. Someone will have to go for one.''

''He's going to have a hell of a headache when he wakes up,'' he said, nodding toward a faint bruise on the old man's temple. ''He must have hit the wall, or an armrest, on his way down.''

''Great. A lawsuit is just what I need.''

Ellery hesitated, unsure what to do next. He could offer to wait with Callum until someone came, but he barely knew him, and Davidson's size—well over six feet, with the weight to go with it—made him feel uncomfortable. He smiled weakly, looked again at the unconscious man on the couch, and went into the lobby as the manager began suggesting that Seth, if he were a truly good human being, should volunteer to fetch the doctor.

When the door closed behind him, he headed for the nearest exit, buttoning his coat, preparing to leave. But he stopped when he saw Katherine Avalon, part owner of the record shop, standing in the middle of the floor, head back, staring up at a huge chandelier whose teardrop crystals were reflecting and amplifying the light from the candelabra set at each of the concession counters and on two of the low Sheraton tables between the couches and chairs.

"Wow," she said excitedly. "Hey, look at this. God, they look just like stars!"

No one moved, and he noted with a puzzled frown that if all the people in the lobby were the only ones who had come to the late show that night, the theater had been a lot more empty than it felt.

There were only six, including a couple sitting on the center couch, and another pair much younger on the far staircase, sharing a cigarette.

Something was wrong.

He glanced back at the office.

Something . . . and he saw it. In the glass doors that led to the street. The black outside.

Jesus, he thought, and walked over to take a look.

In the candleglow that stretched weakly to the curb, he saw the rain—sheets and lashes of it exploding on the pavement, driven in hard slants and silvered cyclones by the wind charging down Park Street, sweeping around the corner, spilling over the theater roof, and slamming against the doors. At times it rattled against the glass like pellets of ice, sending white webs to the frames and obscuring the street; then the wind took another direction, and he saw black rivers rushing high in the gutters.

He turned, pointing behind him in amazement, and let his arm drop.

That's what was wrong.

Not the rain—the people. No one had their coats on; no one was leaving.

Flustered for a moment, and blaming his reaction on Toni's odd behavior, he forced himself with a deep breath to relax, understanding that those who stayed behind were probably hoping the rain would ease soon, or the wind calm down, to give them a chance outside without drowning on their feet. Cozy, he thought then; just like in the movies, where everybody gets to know everybody else, secrets are spilled, murders are committed, and when the sun shines again, the hero and heroine walk off to a new life. He chuckled at the images that formed and re-formed, and decided that he might as well do the same. He took off his coat and wandered over to the nearest refreshment stand, grunted when he saw the clerk had already gone, and jumped when a hand lightly tapped his shoulder.

"Nerves, El?" Katherine said.

He laughed and leaned back against the display case. "Just had a sudden attack of the hungries, that's all."

She patted his stomach and shook a finger at him. "Hungries, at your age, will get you a pot."

"At my age, I'm lucky to get the hungries at all," he answered, not at all sure he was making any sense, and knowing he seldom did when she was around. Ever since he had taken the job to manage Yarrow's a year ago, he had not lost a single opportunity to get a glimpse of her whenever he walked to the luncheonette for his noon meal; he had even, for a stretch of three weeks during the winter, tried to time his arrival on Centre Street with hers. It made him feel like a jerk. And he felt even worse when he twice asked her to dinner and was twice refused—politely, even regretfully—but he hadn't found the courage to ask her out again.

A sudden splash of rain against the doors made her turn around. "I think I'm on the Ark, you know?"

Then Seth came out of the office, bundled in a green plastic poncho, a floppy-brimmed hat, and holding an umbrella a dazzling red. He grimaced comically when Ellery lifted an eyebrow, ignored good-natured jeers from the others, and stood at the exit. Waited. Lifted his shoulders and pushed through, and they flinched at the wind that sailed into the room. Several candles went out, and the rest danced unpleasant shadows on the floor and the walls.

The usher hadn't gone two steps before the storm yanked the umbrella from his hands. There was a brilliant burst of blue-white that turned the rain to silver slashes as he hurried to the curb; and in the afterimage, after Seth had vanished, Ellery was sure the boy had thrown up his hands.

"Christ, will you look at that damned rain," a man said from the couch.

The woman beside him shifted uneasily. "I think we ought to leave now, Gary. It doesn't look like it's going to get any better." She blinked then when she realized the others were watching, and a faint blush darkened her already darkly rouged cheeks. Her husband leaned toward her and lay a hand on her leg. She sat back, her fingers busily twisting a handkerchief, her eyes on the chandelier.

Ellery looked away, embarrassed for the woman's fear and understanding it perfectly. Storms like this were better suffered at home, not in the company of strangers. He leaned his forearms on the top of the glass case and stared at the empty popcorn machine.

Katherine mimicked his stance and whispered, "Paula Richards."

"What?"

"That's Paula Richards," she said, lowering her voice still further.

"No kidding? Of *the* Richards?"

She nodded.

"I'll be damned."

He had never seen any of that family before, knew them only by reputation as a somewhat reclusive clan, and by their address on Williamston Pike, assuming it was one of the estates that lined the road out to the valley. Once a month, at least since he'd worked there, one of the household staff dropped by the store and ordered over a hundred dollars' worth of books. All sorts of books. All in paperback. And once a month, another staff member came by to pick them up.

A quick guilty glance, and he nodded to himself. She was slender, and rather pretty in spite of the severe tweed suit, the unruffled white blouse, the shoes almost large enough to be brogans. The effect was, in fact, almost pathetic, straight out of a Forties' film, the plain-jane clerk waiting for Cary Grant and getting instead the man he'd guessed rightly was her husband, himself in a dark blue tailored suit, and a pair of sneakers that had seen better days.

Again he turned around, leaned back, stuffed his hands in his pockets. Katherine said something before turning as well, and he stared dumbly at her.

"As a cat," she repeated with a gently mocking smile. "As in 'as nervous as.' That's you."

"It shows?"

A wink for a nod. "Bad day?"

"Bad day. Bad week. Bad month. I think I'll go outside and throw myself into the gutter."

Understatement, he thought. The owners of the bookstore had been watching him closely for the past few weeks, doublechecking his bookkeeping without being obvious about it, suggesting more than once—and kindly, he had to admit—that perhaps he might like to take the vacation time he'd accumulated over the year. But he couldn't leave. From home to store to home again he was safe, prevented by his work and his solitude from making the mistakes that had brought him here in the first place. The bumbling, foolish errors that had cost him his previous job, his previous lover, and all jobs and lovers before them. A therapist had told him—no charge, El, you're a friend—he was tailoring his own excuses for running back home from a world that didn't know he existed. He wasn't sure. It didn't matter. He was home, after twenty years, and nothing had changed.

Katherine lay a hand on his arm, stroked it once, and gave him sympathy with a look. Then she tilted her head toward the office door. "Who's the old guy?"

"I don't know. He fell."

"Is he all right?"

"Toni says so. Just hit his head. Seth's gone for—"

"Toni?" she said, eyes wide now and the smile broad. "Toni who?"

"Toni Keane," he answered peevishly, not liking her tone, thinking she knew of his infatuation and was rubbing it in. "She's Doctor Keane's—" He scanned the lobby for her and frowned. "Guess she's in the ladies' room."

The couple on the balcony steps were whispering and passing another cigarette back and forth, and he watched them for a minute, envious of the boy's hand draped casually over her shoulder, the tips of his fingers just brushing across the top of her breast, envious of the girl's self-assurance that didn't force her to drive them away with a pout for convention. The sexual revolution, he thought glumly; only they didn't come by and draft me. The rats.

Davidson stalked out of the office then, scowling, his raincoat on. ''Phone's still out,'' he announced as he slapped a hat on his head. ''Seth's not back. I'll head over to the police, okay, folks? Don't worry about a thing. See you in a minute.''

And he was gone before anyone could say a word, the door wind-slammed behind him, rain spattering in on the carpet, the candles dancing and dying again.

Though Ellery waited for it, half expected it, there was no bolt of lightning. The manager strode through the light, into the black, and all they could hear was the hiss of running water.

''I'll be damned,'' said Gary Richards as he pushed off the couch and walked to the door. ''Can you beat that? He just walked out, just like that. God, some people, you know?''

His wife stood as if to join him, saw Ellery and smiled shyly. When he returned the smile, she walked over hesitantly, nodded politely to Katherine, and said, ''Excuse me, but you . . . you're the man from Yarrow's, aren't you.''

"And you're the lady who's keeping us in business."

Her laugh was high and quiet, though it didn't quite reach to her eyes. "I like to read," she said apologetically. "There isn't much else to do, really." A movement of her hand. "Gary's always busy with this and that and the business. I—" She paused, ducked her head, lifted it again. "He thinks I'm going to ruin my eyes."

"Never," he said. "Look at me. I read all the time, and I'm only half blind."

Paula Richards stared, then laughed again. "I guess we'd better go. We, uh . . . it doesn't look like it's going to stop anytime soon."

"Think of this as a dream," he said as she turned to leave. "Your head or mine."

Again she blinked. "I read about them, you know. Dreams. It's very interesting."

"Yes, you are," and he smiled, wider when she put a hand to her cheek and looked as if, before she turned away, the one thing in the world she wanted to do most was wink at him and grin.

As she walked away, Katherine nudged his side with a soft elbow. "That was very nice."

"She seems like a nice woman."

"So am I when you get to know me," she said, and headed for the ladies' room on the lobby's other side.

He gaped, not caring that he probably looked as if he'd just been punched in the stomach. He wasn't so dense that he missed her intent, but the courage to follow her was blocked by a loud round of swearing. Richards was standing by the lefthand exit, his hands on the glass. Paula was behind him, a palm on his shoulder, pulling him back gently.

"No, damnit!" the man said angrily. "I will not calm down!" He turned to the others, face dark and eyes wide in indignation. Even the couple on the staircase looked at him curiously. "It's locked," Richards announced, kicking back with one heel. Then he pushed his wife to one side and tried the other door. "Damn! I don't believe it! Both of them! I mean . . . that stupid manager's locked us all in."

Ellery doubted it. In the first place, it didn't make any sense to do something like that. In the second place, Davidson simply hadn't had the time; he had just walked out into the storm without stopping, without even turning around. But when Richards saw the expression on his face and challenged him with a look, he tried them himself, leaned down and peered at the tiny gap between door and frame.

"What did I tell you?" Richards said over his shoulder. "The stupid sonofa—"

"It isn't locked," Ellery said, and pointed. "The bolt's not over." When he pushed, however, it didn't give. He pulled, and pulled harder. Pushed a second time and watched as Richards did the same on the other side. "Maybe all the water's warped the frames or something."

"They're aluminum," the man said sarcastically. "How the hell is that gonna warp? Jesus."

"What about the fire exits?"

They turned at the question, saw the boy on the staircase coming down toward them.

"You want to break a leg going in there, Scotty?" Richards said sarcastically as he pointed to the auditorium doors. "It's pitch black, for god's sake. But go ahead, I don't care." He looked at Ellery and rolled his eyes. "The kid's a jerk. He works for his old man, gardening and stuff. The old man couldn't grow sand in a desert."

Ellery said nothing. He didn't know the boy, and right now didn't much care for Gary Richards. He checked the doors again to give himself something to do, knowing it had to be a warp of some kind because doors didn't lock without a bolt turning over, and they sure as hell didn't lock on their own.

Another push for good measure, another pull that nearly wrenched his shoulder, and he went into the office in hopes of finding some sort of clue as to the doors' closing, maybe something to do with new turns in electronics. Scotty was taking the usher's flashlight from a shelf on the wall. They exchanged a look that condemned Richards and, at the same time, forged no abrupt alliances. Then he was gone, and Ellery scratched the side of his nose, rubbed its tip, and knew he was wasting his time. A single candle burned feebly on the desk, and as far as he could tell, there was no exit here. The old man was still on the couch, still unconscious, and snoring. Ellery grinned at him, wished him luck, and returned to the lobby.

The far doors to the auditorium were swinging slowly and soundlessly shut; the young girl was still on the staircase, and she waved to him, grinned, and made a face at Richards. He grinned and waved back, took another step and rubbed his palms briskly. It was getting cold in here, the same flat cold he had felt earlier, and by the expressions on the others, they felt it as well.

The doors stopped swinging.

A fresh fall of rain slapped against the glass, and Paula jumped away as if she'd been drenched. Her husband swore and glared at the pavement, threatening Davidson in absentia and damning the storm in the same breath.

There was thunder. No lightning. The creak of a floorboard, the squeal of a hinge.

Ellery pulled at the bottom of his sport jacket, pulled at his shirt as if he were wearing a tie too tight for his throat. And he watched in amazement as the candles on the refreshment counter across the lobby began to sputter, to smoke, and one by one flare out. It left only six burning, on a table by the wall, and he stared at them, too, waiting for them to die and leave them all in the dark.

As it was, the room pulled in on itself, the light barely reaching the exits, not touching the rain at all. All he could hear then was the hiss, and the slap, the ghosts of the storm scratching to get in.

Ellery pulled back his jacket sleeve and looked at his watch; it was just past eleven. Davidson had left for the police nearly thirty minutes ago, and Scotty had been in the auditorium for just about ten. He considered checking on the boy, but Katherine came out of the rest room and stopped, a hand waving briefly in front of her face until she realized what had happened to the rest of the light. By then he was beside her, explaining quickly about the doors, ignoring the increasingly loud curses Richards was spouting despite his wife's gentle pleading to please stay calm.

Then he heard another voice, plaintive and small. "Scotty?"

It was the girl on the staircase, and without

thinking he climbed three steps to sit in front of her, Katherine climbing two more to kneel at her side.

"Hi," he said. "I'm Ellery Phillips."

She was terrified. Her blonde hair had been ribbon-tied into a pony tail, and she had pulled it over her shoulder to stroke it quickly, hold it, while her free hand rubbed her arm for warmth. When he repeated his name and laid a finger on her knee to get her attention, she glanced fearfully at the auditorium doors, back to him, then to Katherine.

"Ginny," she said, sounding no more than six. "Ginny Amerton."

"Oh, yeah," he said with a mock scowl. "Your dad's been trying to sell me a Mercedes for a zillion years. I keep telling him he'll have to pay for half, and he keeps throwing me out."

The smile for his effort was feeble, but it was a smile nonetheless. "We're trapped in here, right?"

He shook his head immediately. "Ginny, how can you get trapped in a movie theater? Scotty's checking the fire exits, right? And if they're locked like these here, we'll . . ." He looked over his shoulder at Richards pacing the lobby, Paula now slumped on the ticket taker's stool. He lowered his voice. "We'll use the creep over there to break the glass."

Katherine laughed quietly, and poked the girl's arm until she broke and laughed too.

Thunder shook the walls.

Another candle went out.

Ellery exaggerated a groan as he stretched his arms over his head and stood. "Guess I'll go see how Scotty's doing." And with a look asked Katherine to stay behind with the girl. She nodded; he smiled and backed down to the floor, telling himself there was nothing to worry about, all will soon be revealed. When Paula saw him moving and half rose from the stool, he pointed to the doors. She shrugged, and Richards gave no indication he either cared or would join him.

Wonderful, he thought as he pushed into the auditorium; this is just great.

And he thought it again when the door closed silently behind him, and the only light came from a pebbled glass square over his shoulder.

He didn't call out; he didn't want to worry Ginny. Instead, he walked to the head of the center aisle and searched for the flashlight's beam, down at the exits flanking the stage, and on either side of him in the wide corridor that ran behind the seats.

Black; nothing but black. And no response when

he whispered, "Scotty, hey, Scotty!" as loud as he dared.

Christ, the kid probably fell or something, he decided, and made his way along the wall to the lefthand fire door, grabbed the crossbar, and shoved down. It didn't move. When he tried to pull it up, his hands slipped and he nearly fell on his back. The opposite door was the same—iron, sounding hollow when he kicked it, not budging when he put his shoulder to it and pushed as hard as he could. His soles slipped on the worn carpeting. His palms coated the bar with sweat and his fingers lost their grip.

No sweat, he thought; the other ones.

Down the side aisle, then, keeping one hand on the wall and moving slowly in case he met Scotty along the way, speaking the boy's name and damning him for not answering. He probably thought it was a practical joke. He was probably already back in the lobby, and the others were just waiting to yell "Surprise!" when he came out.

The exits were locked.

He glanced toward the lobby doors to reassure himself of the light, then decided he might as well do a little checking on his own as long as he was here. Just don't take too long, he told himself; don't take too long.

But there was nothing on the stage when he

climbed awkwardly up and poked around in the small storage spaces behind the velvet curtains. The screen was fixed to the cinder-block wall behind; there was no room for a door, much less a place for someone to hide.

Damned stupid kid, he thought, dusting off his hands and shirt, hating to think that Richards had been right.

Then he heard a scream, muffled, prolonged, and a sudden babble of voices that sent him leaping to the floor, colliding with a series of armrests until he found the center aisle and charged up. The light from the door window was flickering wildly, and he thought for a moment a fire had broken out—one of the candles had tipped over somehow, igniting the carpet. He was trying to remember if he'd seen a fire extinguisher as he pushed through, and stumbled to a halt.

Gary was standing in front of one of the doors, a chair in his hands. Paula was kneeling on the floor, crying. Katherine and Ginny were waiting at the bottom of the staircase, and it was clear from the girl's face it was she who had screamed.

"What?" he demanded.

Scotty wasn't there.

"What?" Richards said angrily, almost shouting. "Hell, I'll show you what," and he lifted the chair over his head, almost overbalanced before bringing it down on the door.

The glass didn't break.

One of the legs did.

Bewildered, Ellery watched as the man staggered to the door on the right and tried it again, twice, this time sending the seat spinning to the floor. Then he threw the chair as hard as he could against the glass wall of the ticket seller's booth. It trembled, but didn't shatter. As far as Ellery could see, it didn't even crack.

"Scotty," the girl said at last, and they turned one by one. "Where's Scotty? Mr. Phillips, where's Scotty?"

He had no answer to give her, but he began to wonder if this was something more than just a prank. Someone on the outside didn't want them leaving, and he immediately recalled hostage situations he had read about, seen on television, had heard about from customers coming into the store. But it didn't make sense. The only ones here who had any kind of money for things like ransom were the Richards, and by now the street should have been filled with police cars, lights, sirens, with someone from some lunatic paramilitary group making all sorts of demands for the reporters and cameras.

Yet there was nothing out there.

Nothing but the rain, the thunder, the occasional glare of lightning.

And it didn't explain why the glass didn't break.

Oh, god, he thought, and walked over to the door. His breath smoked a circle, and he wiped it away with one finger.

"Somebody? Please, where's Scotty?"

There were no lights at all out there.

The streetlamps were dark, the shops on Centre Street, the houses, even the white globes in front of the police station. No cars passed, no trucks.

He cupped his hands around his eyes and waited for the next bolt, and when it came, he managed not to blink.

Nothing.

No outlines of buildings, no reflections on the road.

The rain, and the curb, and the rushing black water.

He heard footsteps and whirled to see Ginny taking the stairs up two at a time, Katherine with her hand outstretched and looking to him for help. He wanted to shrug, but when Richards continued to do nothing but pace, he trotted over and peered up to the landing where the staircase jogged to the right.

"What happened?"

"She thinks Scotty's hiding up there. She thinks

. . . she's got the idea someone drugged the refreshments and now Scotty's gone off the deep end or something.''

Her voice was barely under control, and when he put a hand to her shoulder, he could see a throbbing at her temple before she brushed at her hair and covered it.

''Maybe we ought to leave her alone,'' he said. ''She'll be back when she can't find him.''

''She could get hurt, El,'' she said. ''That's steep up there. God, suppose she gets to the bottom and falls.''

''Scotty didn't come out,'' he said, hoping it was a question and taking a breath when Katherine shook her head. ''Then maybe he climbed up somehow. He could be trying the doors to the fire escape.'' Then, suddenly, he looked to the stairs and frowned, looked around the lobby and snapped his fingers. ''Toni,'' he said. ''Damn, I forgot all about Toni.''

When she looked puzzled he reminded her of the girl he had mentioned before this all started.

''Sorry. I don't remember.''

He described her.

''Nope. No bells, sorry. She must have left already.''

''But how?'' he said, struggling with frustration. ''The doors, remember?''

"Davidson left. So did that usher. She must have gone out the same way."

He wanted to ask, to demand to know why they couldn't do the same and get the hell home. Instead, he wondered aloud if the young woman wasn't in the ladies' room, until Katherine told him she had been in there alone.

"Oh, Jesus," he said wearily. "Damn, don't tell me she's lying someplace, hurt like Scotty must be. Christ."

Paula was still on the floor, staring into her lap. "The exits are all locked, aren't they."

He wanted to lie, but there was nothing to gain and she would know it anyway. "As far as I can tell, yes. They must be blocked somehow from the outside."

"Great," Richards said bitterly. "Just . . . shit."

"El," Katherine said then. "What the hell's going on?"

"It's my money," Richards said. "That's probably what it is, you know. Any minute now, some asshole is going to pop up through the floor and demand all my money and a fast plane to Cuba." He wrestled off his tie and tossed it aside. "Dumb shit. Who the hell does he think he is?"

Ellery didn't say a word, not surprised the man had come to the same conclusion he had, though he knew it wasn't right, not right at all.

The night was too dark, and . . . he shuddered, exhaled, and exhaled again when he thought he saw the ghost of his breath. A third time proved him wrong, but the cold didn't leave him.

"El?" Katherine said. "El, please, what's going on? Is he right? Is that what it is?"

"I don't know." And he wished they would stop looking to him for answers. He didn't know anything, and he didn't know how to find out, but for the time being, to keep himself from thinking too much, he could get Ginny back here with the rest, and maybe find Toni in the bargain.

Taking one of the candles then, and hissing when a drop of wax landed on his wrist, he cupped his hand around the flame and started up. Katherine moved to go with him, paused halfway to the landing, and changed her mind with a nervous smile. When he reached the turn and looked down, she had already gone back to Paula and was helping her to the couch. He couldn't see Gary at all, only heard him kicking at the pieces of the chair he had broken.

Insane, he thought as he rounded the corner and started up the second flight; it's crazy.

"Ginny!"

At the top of the stairs was a narrow passageway. It ran the width of the building and, like the floor below, had a low wall on the left, broken in

182

the center and both ends for the step-aisles down. The righthand wall was blank save for a pair of large-framed wildlife prints that needed a good dusting.

"Toni?"

There was thunder.

"Toni Keane, where are you? Are you okay?"

He looked down the side aisle, lifting his shoulders against the wintery cold, lifting the candle high and away from his eyes.

"Ginny, c'mon, answer me! He's not up here. C'mon!"

To the center aisle, a draught snaking about his ankles, and he stepped through the gap, took the first step down, and felt his temper begin to flare.

"Toni! Ginny! What the hell's going on?"

Shifting his fingers to escape a run of hot wax. Keeping his face slightly averted so not to be blinded by the white of the flame and the halo around it.

"Damnit, Ginny, will you show yourself for god's sake?"

Another step, and a third.

Candlelight shimmered shadows across the empty seats, shifting them back and forth, raising the far end of the row and rolling the backs toward him like gelid waves in a black sea. It was a dizzying effect, and he closed his eyes for a moment, opened them, and saw the girl pressed against the far wall. Her hands were out to the sides, her eyes so wide he could see nothing but white, and her shirt was pulled out of the waistband of her jeans.

"Jesus, Ginny," he said, not bothering to disguise his relief. He made his way along a row toward her, holding the candle higher. "Jesus, why the hell didn't you answer me, huh? You've got me scared half to death." He tried a laugh and gave it up, shifted the candle into his left hand, and ignored a sudden sharp burning at the base of his thumb. "You haven't seen Toni, have you? No, of course not. You don't even know her. Look, why don't you just—"

Her head began rocking slowly side to side, her outstretched arms were trembling, but she didn't move, didn't speak, and it hit him that she might have found Scotty after all; from the terror she showed him, it wasn't going to be nice.

His attention snapped then to the floors between the rows, but he couldn't see anything down there but a few crushed cigarette butts, burnt matches, an empty box of popcorn, a half-filled paper cup of soda, another one on its side.

And his own shadow darting into the gaps, darting away, disappearing.

He could hear her breathing when he was halfway along—harsh, quick, prelude to a scream.

"Take it easy," he said quietly. "Take it easy, Ginny, it's only me."

He moved again, watching her head rock faster and faster while her legs began to palsy, one heel thumping hollow against the baseboard. Softly, then loudly, and softly again. Her gaze shifting into puzzled focus on his face, her lips quivering for a moment before closing. He smiled at her and checked the rows above and below him, seeing nothing at all until he saw her feet. They were bare, and he realized she had stopped drumming on the wall.

"Okay, Ginny," he said. And stopped.

She had relaxed, and somehow the ribbon from her ponytail had come undone and was draped now over one shoulder, almost lost in the spray of her dark blonde hair. The shirt was open three buttons down, exposing pale breasts against a tanned chest and a small white rose in the center of her bra.

He heard a soft click, looked down, and saw a button bounce on the floor and roll out of sight.

"Ginny, what's—"

The shirt was completely open, and she hadn't moved her hands. The snap of her jeans was undone, the plane of her stomach gold in the candlelight, pushing slowly out, sighing slowly in.

"Ginny," he said harshly, damning his shadow

now growing on the wall, covering her, shading her bronze. "Ginny, where is Scotty? Can you tell me where Scotty is? Is he hurt?"

She smiled at him, innocence and seduction. Her jeans were crumpled at her feet, and the shirt slipped over her shoulder while he watched, hissing when it caught at her waist, hissing again when it slid to the floor. He turned away as if looking for someone to witness what was happening here, turned back to see her reach her arms out toward him. Reluctantly, he stepped closer, shaking his head at her, trying by his expression to tell her she didn't know what she was doing.

Wax poured onto his hand, and he cursed, dropped the candle, and the flame died on the wick.

"Goddamn," he muttered, raising an angry fist toward the girl, lowering it slowly when he realized he could still see her. The candle was out. The light hadn't gone. It still lay his hovering shadow over her face, still coated her with colors the flame never had.

Hallelujah, he thought; someone's finally fixed the electricity.

"Okay, kiddo," he said sternly. "Let's stop the nonsense, all right? They'll be coming up to see how you are, and I don't want them to find you like this. So look, do us both a big favor and pick up—''

He had turned to hurry back along the row to the center aisle, and said no more when he saw the exit signs over the fire doors still unlit, the bulbs recessed in the ceiling still dark. A hand grabbed for a seat back. The balcony was black except where he stood.

''Ellery,'' Ginny whispered, not the voice of a girl.

He ordered himself not to look.

''Ellery.''

He didn't understand the light, but he knew full well what the girl wanted, what she was trying to do. Her mind had snapped, no question about it, probably from something she had stumbled on up here, something he hadn't yet seen himself. And if he looked now, he would only encourage her; if he turned, he wouldn't know how to get her dressed again without using force, and he knew what that would look like should anyone come up to see what was taking him so long in his search.

''Ellery.''

''Ginny, for Christ's sake, would you knock it off and—''

Her hand gripped his shoulder and twisted viciously, until he either had to turn or sprawl over the chairs. His jacket tore at the seam as if it were paper, his shirt tore as well, and there was a fire along his skin that made him hiss and yank free, stumbling back until he grabbed an armrest and steadied.

"Ellery."

Her eyes were dull orange, her teeth lengthened to fangs, her hair was a nest of spitting black serpents.

He screamed and his left arm lashed out, catching her on the temple and tumbling her into the next row, where she regained her feet before he could turn and run, snakes gone, eyes normal, teeth covered by lips that were shining with the blood streaming from her nose.

She smiled. "Ellery."

And she was naked.

"Ellery."

She climbed agilely over the seat after him, grinning as he backed away while holding his aching shoulder, giggling when he held out a palm to stop her as if he were staving off a vampire with a large silver cross. Then she shuddered, straightened, and ran her hands up her sides until they were cupping her breasts, kneading them, flattening them, slipping one hand down over her stomach, up again, slowly, smearing her blood in pale patterns across her amber skin. Holding out a hand, stretching out a finger, reaching for him, to touch him, before he spun around and tried to run, tripped into the aisle and fell. His head struck a riser, and he grunted in pain; he blinked rapidly to clear his eyes and rolled onto his back.

She was standing over him.

Straddling him.

Bending down in the nonlight until he saw the flesh peeling patches from her cheeks, her forehead, the sides of her nose.

He screamed when she reached for him, her hands nothing but bone that cracked at the joints; screamed again when she took hold of his belt and lifted his hips effortlessly off the floor.

Screamed a third time when she smiled, and the light snapped out.

He assumed he had fainted, blacked out for a second, maybe two, when the thing that was Ginny Amerton hauled his groin toward her teeth. And when consciousness returned, he flailed hysterically at the air, twisting onto a hip, kicking out, grunting, feeling tears in his eyes until, at last, he calmed and lay cheek-down on the steps, gulping for a breath and telling himself over and over and over again that he was all right, he was all right, he was alone up here and he was all right. Something had somehow triggered an hallucination, but he was all right now, and he could stand if he tried.

"All right," he said to hear the sound of his voice. "You're all right, pal. No sweat. Get up and get moving before they think you're dead."

His legs weren't listening. They refused to hold him, the muscles jumping in spasms until he had to grab for an armrest and hauled himself to his knees. Lowered his head. Panted again for air. Ignoring the dark while he listened for footsteps, for the rub of fleshless hand over cloth, over wood, for someone other than himself in the balcony's night.

What he heard was thunder; what he felt was the floor vibrating until the thunder was gone.

He stood at last, not knowing how long it had taken for him to do it without falling down again; he used the seats to pull himself painfully up the aisle, not knowing how he managed to find the strength even to hold on; he used the wall to keep from falling and eventually made it to the top of the staircase, checking behind him twice every step of the way while he talked himself into believing he had imagined the whole thing. And talked again, commanded, when his hands began to shake, so badly his wrists and knuckles began to ache. And a third time when he knew that unless someone talked to him, and talked to him soon, he was going to cry.

If only, he thought, it wasn't so damned dark!

Five minutes while he leaned against the wall and felt the blood on his shoulder and the sweat on his face; and five again while he stared at the faint light on the landing below him. He didn't bother to wonder why he couldn't hear the others, only drinking in the sight like heady gulps of fresh spring air. Calming. Real. No threat or nightmare there.

God, he thought; Jesus God.

He swallowed dryly and coughed, then gripped the banister white-knuckled until he reached the turn. There was silence below, but he forced himself to wait, to claw fingers through his hair, to pull off the jacket and brush a palm over his shirt. Then he stepped around the corner, smiling grimly, eyes narrowed.

The lobby was empty.

Katherine and Paula weren't on the couch, and when he staggered down to the carpet, he couldn't find Gary.

No, he thought; no. They couldn't have gotten out and forgot me. They couldn't!

"Hey, Katherine!" he called as he hurried to the exit. "Mrs. Richards?"

The doors still wouldn't open, the remains of the battered chair still scattered by the ticket booth.

"Katherine?"

The rain washing the glass, the wind bringing in the cold.

"Paula? Gary?"

The office door was open, and he started toward it in a rush, slowed, and moved cautiously though he wasn't sure why. And every step he took, he expected Ginny to leap out at him, shrieking with laughter, the flesh still falling from her skeleton and the blood still running from her nose.

The chandelier trembled; the crystals rang like tiny bells that had never been tuned.

"Look, guys," he said as he stepped over the threshold.

The office was empty, except for the injured man still sleeping on the couch. The candle burning on the desk was much lower, and he could see the bruise on the man's temple darkening, spreading, as if there was hemorrhaging. He hurried over and shook his shoulder, shook it harder when there was nothing but a waggling of the man's head. Holy shit, he thought, and knelt beside him, put a finger to his neck, to his wrist, to find evidence of a heartbeat. It was there, but it was weak, and he licked at his lips as he returned to the lobby.

"I don't get it," he said aloud, hands on his

hips. "Hey, Katherine! Mrs. Richards? Paula?"
He pushed the auditorium door in and braced it
open with one foot. "Gary! Hey, Richards, where
the hell are you guys, huh?"

Nothing in there but the dark; even the huge
screen had stopped its glowing.

It's all right, he told himself. It's cool, it's all
right, they'll be back.

He backed into the lobby and watched the door
swing silently shut. A nightmare, he decided; Ginny,
the rain—it's a goddamned nightmare, that's all.

Ellery

He whirled to stare at the staircase he'd taken,
whirled again to peer at the one on his right. No
one was there; no shadows, no nightmare.

But he noticed the men's room door and rushed
in, propped it open with a trash can to give him
feeble light, and called again for Richards, shut-
ting up instantly when the name echoed flatly off
the dull white tiles. The three stall doors were
open; water dripped from one of the faucets; a
shred of brown paper towel dangled from its dis-
penser and waved at him in a draught. The stench
of stale disinfectant gagged him; the smell of his
own sweat was sour and strong.

Without thinking, not daring to think, he crossed
to the sink and turned the faucet off with an angry
twist, yanked away the strip of toweling and used

it to dry his hands, tore off another length and soaked it in warm water. He rinsed his face, dried it, dried his hands twice, all the while avoiding a look at his reflection in the mirror above the basin. He was not a brave man, and was not ashamed to admit it; and he knew that as soon as he saw the look on his face, the look in his eyes, something inside was going to shatter.

He sighed explosively, and moved on his toes to the door so not to have to hear his footsteps.

A look at his watch; it was well past midnight.

A look to the outside; it was still raining hard.

It wasn't until he found himself staring at the candles on the table that he realized he would have to do something soon or they were all going to go out at about the same time; and when they did, he would be alone. In the dark.

Quickly, he pinched out the flames of all but one, sagged into a chair, and stared blindly at the front doors. A single candle wasn't much, but four of them would last a hell of a lot longer one at a time. By then, if he were lucky, it would be daylight and he'd be able to signal someone out on the street to get help, to let him out.

But Davidson had left, and so had Seth and Toni, and in all the time they'd been gone, not one had returned.

Ellery

He ignored it. It was only his nerves playing stupid games.

"I will wake up now," he said loudly, pleased his voice didn't crack or waver. "I will wake up *now*, and I will go home."

It had been a boring film.

"Now! I am waking up right now!"

He couldn't even remember the title, and he had fallen asleep somewhere in the middle, drained because of the problems at the store, weary because he couldn't seem to get his personal life in line, disgusted because he had no one to blame but himself. Every morning without exception, he woke up determined to take charge; and most evenings he returned home, thinking that perhaps his brother during their last meeting two years ago had been right, that he was a loser. Not because he wasn't smart, but because he allowed too many people to have too great a say in what should be his destiny, his own fate.

"I *will* wake up," he said to the empty lobby.

"Then can I wake up too?" Katherine asked him, leaning against the frame of the ladies' room door, her makeup smeared, her eyes red from weeping.

When he spoke her name, his breath was white. When he took off his jacket to place around her shoulders, a fresh flow of blood stained the sleeve of his white shirt.

When she asked him what happened, he only looked at the stairs.

"Did your brother really call you a loser?"

They were on the couch, his arm around her shoulders, and they were staring at the rain.

He hadn't realized he had been speaking aloud, and he answered her truthfully, making her frown.

"He was wrong, then, wasn't he," she said.

"I guess. I don't know. Sometimes I wonder."

She snuggled closer, laying her head on his shoulder as she drew up her legs, not bothering to adjust the skirt that exposed most of a thigh. He touched her hair. She sighed and told him that not long after he had gone upstairs after Ginny, Richards had decided he and his wife would do what Ellery was obviously incapable of doing—find a way out. The man, she said, had virtually dragged his wife into the auditorium, and when they hadn't returned after fifteen minutes or so, she had gone in to check on them. They were gone. She had called to Ellery from the middle aisle, but he hadn't answered. She could not, however, bring herself to go up the stairs, so she'd gone into the rest room instead. Hidden. And started to cry.

"I want to know what's going on."

"So do I. Believe me, so do I."

"But there has to be a reason!"

"I know, I know."

And he told her about his earlier notion it might be some sort of hostage situation, though not the kind Richards had claimed, or a prank, or maybe someone was out there fiddling around with electronics, which might explain why the doors wouldn't open and the telephone wouldn't work. He knew next to nothing about such things, and could not explain, when asked, why the glass wouldn't break. Nor could he explain what had happened to Ginny.

"Now that has to be a trick," she said in disgust, shivering in spite of the fact he hadn't told her the whole story. "I mean, that kind of weird stuff just doesn't happen."

"Except in dreams," he said quietly.

Without warning she pinched his chest hard and he yelped, almost slapped her when she pinched him again. "Not a dream," she said. "So what the hell is it?"

By his reckoning it wasn't more than fifteen minutes before they roused themselves from the couch in a tacit decision to make a methodical search of the building for the others, and for a way out.

They didn't talk about the storm; they didn't react to the lightning and thunder.

By consent, they began in Davidson's office, not bothering to remain quiet despite the old man's restless sleep. Drawers were opened, emptied, and were empty of keys; they could find no tools, no extra flashlights, nothing on any of the papers they uncovered that would tell them what had gone wrong with the theater tonight. The rug was turned up wherever they could move it, furniture was shifted, a storage closet was found that was completely empty. They tapped the walls for hidden exits, feeling like fools and doing it twice again. He climbed on a chair to tap the ceiling for a trapdoor entrance to a crawlspace or attic; and she stared at the old man for over a full minute, finally leaned down and shouted in his ear, slapped his face hard, and was about to drag him to the floor when Ellery stopped her, grabbing her in his arms and taking her gently out.

"Who *is* he?"

"I don't know."

"Where did he come from?"

"I don't know that either. I just found him, that's all."

"The sonofabitch. I hope he dies."

They searched the rest rooms again, propping

open the doors to let some of the candlelight creep
in before them.

They each took one of the staircases to the
balcony, felt their way along the upstairs wall, and
met in the middle. He almost didn't make it. He
couldn't look down the aisles, and when Katherine
asked him where he had last seen the girl, he
couldn't even lift a finger to point. It was too dark
up here, darker than it should have been, and it
was all he could do to keep from grabbing her and
screaming.

In the lobby he hefted the ticket seller's stool
and prodded the doors with its thin metal legs,
harder each time as frustration shortened his breath
and turned his muscles rigid, until he was ram-
ming furiously against the glass, in the corners, in
the center, while the rain ran in white-edged sheets
and the thunder mocked him and the lightning
showed him nothing but his reflection in its glare.
His hair darkened with perspiration, his lips were
drawn back, teeth bared, tongue flicking; a leg
buckled and he was thrown forward, hitting his
shoulder against the jamb, and he whirled and
threw the stool across the room, shouting wordlessly,
fists in the air, then at his temples. Then down at
his sides.

Katherine reached into a display case and tossed
him a box of candy. He let it bounce off his chest,

staring at it dumbly until she picked it up, took his arm, and pulled him down to the floor. She opened the package and gave him a piece.

"It's chewy," she said. "It'll help calm you."

Her hair was in rags across her face, and no matter how often she pushed it away, it returned. Her blouse was stained wet and bunched over her waistband, and somewhere along the line she had tossed the suit's jacket onto the couch.

"I think," she said at last, "this is a judgment of some kind."

His mouth was filled with tasteless candy, but he chewed it anyway, swallowing, sometimes choking.

"I mean, it could be, couldn't it? Like we've been transported somehow to a different plane than the one we live on—you know what I mean? Do you know about planes? Of existence?" He nodded; she nodded back. "So we're here, see, and we're being judged. Like we're already dead. We don't know it, but we are." She grinned. "You must have had some pretty interesting thoughts about women, El, to see Ginny that way."

He spat the candy out behind him, took off his jacket, unbuttoned his shirt, and pulled it down and back roughly to show her his left shoulder. There was a deep, ragged scratch there, and bits of stained white thread sticking to dried blood. "That's not on another plane,'' he told her sharply, pulling the shirt back on and trying not to wince. ''That's here, Katherine. She wasn't an apparition. I saw her. I felt her. She was nothing like a ghost or some kind of an illusion.''

''But she had to be, El. Don't be silly. You must have cut yourself when you tripped on the stairs, caught it on the edge of a seat or something.''

''I fell later, not then.''

She looked down at her shoes. A finger poked at her skirt, flicked at some lint he couldn't see. ''You don't think it's a judgment, then?''

''I don't think so, no.''

''Then what?''

''If I knew that, we'd be gone, don't you think?''

The strain worked on her face, giving her lines about the mouth and canyons beneath her eyes; smudges of dust hollowed her cheeks and streaked over her brow, and though she had tried to wipe away the results of her weeping, flecks of eye shadow and mascara still clung to her skin.

She's beautiful, he thought, and didn't know the question was coming until his lips moved: ''Why didn't you go out with me, Katherine?''

She was startled and leaned away for a second, and he was embarrassed and tried to wave it all aside, telling her with his gestures that it didn't matter, he was being ridiculous, and this was, after all, hardly the time.

"I think," she said, "it was because I felt a little sorry for you."

"You did?"

A nod, a brief smile. "You were trying so hard, El, all those accidental meetings on the street, looking in the store window like you were an urchin begging for food."

"Me?" He didn't know whether to be angry or hurt.

"I didn't want to feel sorry for you, you understand? I wanted to like you without having to feel as if I had to mother you to get your attention." She grinned, like a child who has a wonderful secret. "When you stopped it, I thought you found another girl. Then, when I found out—"

"You found out?"

She shrugged. "I asked around."

It was his turn to grin, and feel awfully foolish.

"When I found out you didn't have a girl, I couldn't get the nerve to call you. Stupid, you know? I wanted to—it's the thing we women can do these days—and I just couldn't do it."

"I'll be damned."

Candlelight danced, and the chandelier sang off-key.

There was no doubt about it—he could see his breath now.

And he didn't move when she said, "There's someone in the theater."

He had heard it almost as soon as she had spoken—a low moaning, someone in pain. Instantly, he was on his feet, grabbing her arm and pulling her with him, telling her to hold the doors open while he went inside, following his shadow to the head of the center aisle and seeing, halfway down, a figure sprawled on the floor. He ran to it without thinking, turned it over, and saw Paula staring back at him, terrified. She began crying the moment she recognized him, threw her arms around his neck when he lifted her and carried her back to the couch. Katherine hovered, and sat beside her on the edge of a cushion as soon as he moved away, helplessly waving his hands until he returned to the auditorium and shouted Gary's name. He knew there would be no response, but he kept it up for several minutes, walking up and down the aisles, ignoring the dark that reached out from the stage to drag him back, drag him under, to where the thunder was born.

Ignoring it as long as he could, too angry to yield to the fear lying in ambush, too frightened to dare let his mind out of its cage.

And when at last he returned to the lobby,

wiping his face dry with a sleeve, Paula was sitting up and Katherine was leaving the ladies' room, a wad of damp paper towel cupped in her hand. She gave him a *she's all right* smile and returned to the couch, daubing Paula's cheeks, her forehead, until her hand was gently pushed away.

"I'll live," she said. "I got scared in the dark and ran. I think I must have collided with a seat or something." And she looked at Ellery. "Is Gary back yet?"

"No. Look, where were . . . no."

"That's okay." She massaged her forearm absently. "He will be. He doesn't like to leave me alone for very long. He says I could hurt myself because I don't pay attention to what I'm doing. He calls me a hothouse flower." A sigh; a deep breath. "Hothouse flowers are stronger than he thinks."

"Why"—Katherine rose and smoothed her skirt down over her hips—"why don't we check the doors again, huh? God knows there isn't anything else—"

"It's still raining," Paula whispered, wonder softening the hysteria in her voice. "It's still pouring out there, and it isn't even flooded."

When she stopped, her teeth began chattering.

"Good idea," he said to Katherine. "We'll each take a candle and make the rounds. There's got to be something we've missed. Maybe some sort of special emergency exit, one of those flush-to-the-wall doors or something.''

He picked up a candle from the table, lighted it, and handed it over. Paula shook her head when he offered her one, pushing back into the couch's corner and holding her arms tight at her sides. Her rouge was gone; there was no blood in her face. Then Katherine headed for the auditorium, stopped, and turned. He was still at the table, looking at the staircases. He couldn't go up there again, not a third time. He didn't care if the place was falling down on their heads, there was nothing anyone could say that would make him climb up there again.

She gave him a smile, pity or sympathy, he didn't know, and he felt no guilt at all when she hurried away, one hand sliding up the brass banister, her shoes at the bottom where she'd kicked them off.

He shook himself to dispell the chill that seemed to deepen for a moment, and winked confidently at Paula before stepping out of the lobby. She whispered something to him—he thought it was *i wish gary were more like you*—but he didn't go back to find out. Whatever it was, it was meant kindly, to be reassuring, and he didn't want to tell her that if Gary were like him, he and his wife would be living someplace far different than their estate on the Pike.

He kept his arm straight out in front of him, the candle at an angle to drop the scalding wax on the floor.

He tried all the doors, pulled aside the wall coverings and examined every inch of brick he could reach, climbed a second time to the stage and hunted for a rear exit he might have overlooked before. All he found was some incomprehensible equipment thrust into the corners, and when he came around the curtain, he glanced up at the balcony to see how Katherine was doing.

There was no light.

He called to her.

There was no answer.

Deciding she had already finished, he moved toward the lobby, thinking about what he'd imagined Paula Richards had said, wondering at the same time why he hadn't panicked. This was, he told himself sardonically, hardly your ordinary predicament, yet he had somehow managed to keep relatively calm, reasonably in control, despite the encounter with. . . . He moistened his lips. He couldn't say it. But there must be something inside him, something he hadn't been able to put to his tongue yet that knew what was happening, or had a fairly good idea; and that influence, felt and not known, must be what was preventing him from dropping off the deep end.

He hurried into the lobby.

He dropped the candle on the floor.

"Oh, god," he said dully. "Oh, my god."

Katherine was sprawled on the carpet under the chandelier, one leg pulled under the other, one hand outstretched and clawed at the air. A candelabrum was lying beside her head, and the left side of her face was covered in red.

"Jesus, Paula, what happened?"

He ran to the fallen woman and put out a hand, drew it back into a fist when he realized she was dead, that the blood on her cheek was already drying.

"Paula, goddamnit, what the hell happened?"

There were tears in his eyes when he looked over his shoulder, and one of them slipped to his cheek when he saw her sitting primly in the middle of the couch. She was looking at her hands folded neatly in her lap, and she was smiling.

It came at last, the scream.

It tightened his chest with bands of cold iron, flexed the muscles of his arms, brought darkred ridges to the sides of his neck.

He looked up to the domed ceiling and saw the nodding shadow of Paula's head, the crystals on the chandelier refusing the light—and he opened his mouth to let out the anger, to set free the fear, to demand in the wailing the explanation rightfully his, for his torment and the dying and the dark that was spilling down the staircase and across the flowered carpet.

In spite of the candles, the dark was closing in.

The concession stands vanished. The steps were gone in black.

And the scream became raw as he tasted blood in his mouth, the sweat pouring down his face, the bite of a split knuckle as the scream settled to a sobbing, to a whimpering, to a harsh and halting breathing that soon dropped him to his back.

And when that stopped as well, he could hear the old man, and the old man was snoring.

"Shit!" he yelled, pounded the floor with both fists and rolled over, scrambled to his feet and felt his eyes widen. "Shit!" as he charged into the office and looked down, his shirt torn off his injured shoulder, his legs snapping outward, trying to hold him while his hands reached for the wattled throat and halted less than a finger's length away.

"Get up!" he screamed.

"Fucking bastard, get up!" he shouted, and threw the weathered coat aside, grabbed the man's lapels and yanked him toward his face. Spittle flew when he screamed again; the head bobbed and nodded when he shook the man furiously; a drop of blood landed on a bruised cheek when he bit into his own lip and threw the old man down.

The eyelids didn't flutter.

The face muscles didn't twitch.

A hand coated with liver spots dangled to the floor.

Rain drummed in cadence; thunder drifted away.

Behind him, so softly, he could hear Paula humming.

"Damn you," he said to the stranger sleeping on the couch, and dropped to his knees, too weak to tear out the old man's throat, to pummel his chest, to drag him into the lobby and break a chair or a table or his own hands over the head that no longer moved.

He sniffed, and the tears stopped, and when the candle on the desk finally guttered out in a draught, he remembered a rhyme and knew then it was so.

"Wake up," he whispered. "Old man, wake up."

Thunder rattled a picture frame on the wall, and the candle flared again, turned to smoke, and the smoke was a shadow.

"Please. Wake up."

He rocked back onto his heels, pushed himself to his feet, and left. Paula was still on the couch.

Katherine's body was gone, and her shoes by the far staircase, the candelabrum, the stains of her blood.

With thumbs pressed to his cheeks, fingers massaging his brow, he walked to the lefthand door and stared out at the rain.

"Paula?"

He could see her in the glass. Pale there as well, her hair fleeing its pins in slow-waving wisps. She was watching him; she had heard him.

"Do you . . ."

The cold drifted from the door, touched him, moved on.

". . . do you remember before, when we were talking about dreams?"

After several seconds she nodded. He didn't ask the next question. He waited instead, until she licked her lips several times and made a feeble effort to put her errant hair to rights. A hand to her throat, pulling the skin thoughtfully, inadvertently loosening the high collar's pearl button. The other hand spread in a fan across her chest.

"We all do it," the reflection said though the dark lips didn't move. "We remember sometimes; we forget most of the time."

Yeah, he thought; but you have nightmares just the same.

"They don't always make sense, except to some

part of your brain.'' A brief scowl, a briefer smile. ''You're supposed to be working out your daily problems somehow.''

Right, he thought; but it doesn't always work.

''Do you dream, Ellery?''

He nodded.

''So do I. It's lovely.''

Raining harder, and easing, until the thunder brought it back.

''I read once,'' she said, ''that you do most of your dreaming, the serious stuff, I mean, just before you wake up.'' A shake of her head; a sighing look at the chandelier. ''I don't know about that. I'm no expert.''

''I know,'' he said, and knew she hadn't heard him.

She continued to talk, and he continued to watch the rain, flaring brightly at times like static on a black screen, drops running together in a mockery of tears.

The cold deepened.

The thunder was gone.

Then he heard Gary's name, and he turned as slowly as his legs would allow.

Paula was standing, her eyes closed, lips parted.

He watched without fascination as her hips thickened slightly beneath the confines of the tweed skirt, her waist draw in, her breasts enlarge, the

211

angles of her face sharpen here, and there grow soft;

he watched as the skirt slit up one side and her leg poked through, the stockings gleaming in the light;

he watched her shoulders broaden, her neck slightly lengthen, her hair break free into a cloud about her head;

he watched tendrils of steam lift from her soles and curl up her spine to slip over her shoulders.

She came toward him, and he met her in the center of the room, the solitary candle behind her not giving her a shadow.

"Paula," he said.

And she spat in his face.

it's raining

He took the seat of the chair Gary had broken a hundred years ago and turned it over, tipped the candle he was holding until a thick puddle of wax gathered on the wood bottom. He held the candle in it until the wax hardened, then placed the seat in front of the door.

When he was sure it wouldn't tip, he walked into the office and checked the old man again, his lips in a spare smile when he was satisfied the man was alive, still breathing.

Paula was gone.

She had run into the auditorium, and he hadn't chased her to bring her back; she was still altering her appearance out of the wallflower mold, and he didn't want to know what she would look like at the end.

it's pouring

The dark was still gathering, and the cold turned his breath to a dead white fog.

You're out there, he thought to the village beyond the dark; goddamnit, I know you're out there.

He sat beside the candle and crossed his legs, pulling his jacket over his shoulders in hope of some warmth.

the old man is snoring

Ginny was wrong—this wasn't some test of experimental drugs some idiot had put in the soda or candy.

Gary was wrong—this wasn't a macabre way to get at his fool money.

he hit his head

And Katherine was wrong, and she was too terribly right—it wasn't a dream that belonged to any of them. If it was true, it belonged to the old man sleeping now in Callum's office; and if Paula was right, the hardest part of dreaming didn't come until the end.

All he could do now was wait, and watch the storm, and wonder without answers why the others had been discarded, one by one, why he had been left to live the last hour of dream time, the dreadful hour at the end before the dreamer awoke.

and he went to bed

He sat then, and he waited, and he tried not to think that maybe he was wrong too.

That maybe it wasn't the old man, that it was him after all.

The candle went out.

Rain ticked against the glass.

And he would not close his eyes when the dark swept around him and he could no longer hear the old man in the office.

He would not close his eyes.

"I am here," he said softly to the rain and took a breath. "I am awake. I am."

and he won't get up till morning

Part Four

Screaming, in the Dark

*E*vening comes rapidly when the year begins to die—when the leaves have all turned and the grass bows against the wind and there's no memory of spring despite the gold left behind by the sun in its setting.

Evening comes, not with shadows but a slow killing of the light . . . and when the light has gone, the trees grow larger and streets become tunnels and porches on old houses no longer hold the swings and the rockers and the warm summer calls to come away, come and sit, and watch for a while.

And when the sidewalks are empty and the cars

have all been parked and the only sign of movement is a leaf scratching at the curb, there are the
sounds, the nightsounds, the last sounds before the
end—of wings dark over rooftops, of footsteps
soft around the corner, of something clearing its
throat behind the hedge near the streetlamp where
white becomes a cage and the shadows seldom
move.

There are stars.

There is a moon.

There are late August wishes and early June
dreams that slip out of time and float into the cold
that turns dew to frost and hardens the pavement,
gives echoes blade edges and makes children's
laughter seem too close to screams.

In the evening; never morning.

When the year begins to die.

The hospital on King Street faces south toward
the woods that flank the Station solidly no matter
how many streets are made. It is three stories high,
tinted windows and brick; a double row of evergreens reaches above the roof, keeping a year-
round screen between the hospital and all its
neighbors. All the patients' rooms are ranged along
the outside walls, to give them views of green; all
the floors except the basement are divided left to
right by a long central corridor that, like the oth-

ers, is tiled and painted in the warmest earth tones, to keep voices and anxieties down and to give visitors the impression the building is much larger than it looks from the curb.

It is seldom full.

It is always fully staffed.

But in spite of the equipment more advanced than most cities, and in spite of the residents, who usually smiled and were usually relaxed and were usually better trained than their counterparts on the outside, Michael suspected that dungeons and medieval prisons were a lot like this: a window you could see through, but too far away to reach even with mighty efforts—a deliberate reminder that freedom was out there and you were still in here, even if your doctor was a genius and your nurse a beauty queen; something to lie on, uncomfortable and hard—a thinly padded rack sadistically designed to put crooks in your back and scabs on your heels and a giggling mad desire to throw yourself on the floor where at least you could sleep without waking slick with sweat; the food in small portions less than fit for human consumption; and the captain of the guards out patrolling the halls, left free by the king to torture the inmates.

No wonder the Bastille had been stormed during the best of the revolution; no wonder they screamed when someone mentioned the Bloody Tower.

On the other hand, he could be dead.

With a sigh for the dubious blessings of mortality, he clasped his hands behind his head, wriggled his buttocks vigorously in a reminder not to get bedsores, and stared glumly at his left leg, invisible in a great white cast putting a dent in the bed. And at his right leg, tucked under the sheet but swollen twice its size from the bandages wrapped around his calf. He twitched the muscles to be sure they still worked, then shifted his gaze to the ceiling.

Brother, he thought glumly.

Softly tan, like the walls; restful perhaps, but without the game-playing flaws he could turn into twisted faces and monsters. Boring. Soporific. As bad as the small television on the wall across the room. The remote-control unit was on the bedtable, but he seldom used it anymore. He hated the game shows. He didn't understand the soap operas. And it seemed that every time someone ran a large piece of equipment somewhere in the building, the picture broke up into colorful, painful static.

Another look at his leg, and he glared at the toes poking through the end of the cast. He wiggled them. He wished someone would come in and tickle them. He wished someone would come in and tickle his side, or under his arms. He wished someone would come in and put a bullet through his head.

One week in this bed and, according to his doctor, probably another week more.

"This," he said aloud, "is boring!"

The varnished pine door to the hallway was propped open, and a nurse stepped in the moment he opened his mouth. She grinned and shook her head in mock despair, and wheeled a small cart to his side, picked up his left hand, and curled her fingers around his wrist.

"You really don't have the right attitude, Mr. Kolle," she scolded lightly with a glance at the gold-framed watch pinned to her chest.

"My attitude," he said, "is rotten because I am bored, Janey. I am bored out of my mind and I want to go home."

She dropped the wrist, picked up an electronic thermometer unit from the cart, and gestured to him. He opened his mouth, and they waited until the unit beeped.

"You dip that in garlic, right?" he said, licking his lips and grimacing.

"Just for you, Mike, just for you."

His next sigh was world-weary as she checked the cast and thumped it with a knuckle, then moved to his right, flipped over the sheet and checked the bandages for loosening. He guessed her to be a good decade younger than he, her hair blonde, her face round, with a height that couldn't have been much above five feet. She worked with a minimum of excess motion and not another word, long fingers deft and delicate, and he could have wept with joy when, as she walked around the foot of the bed, she tickled his toes.

At the cart she checked for medication, found none was required and started out. At the threshold she paused, snapping her fingers. "I forgot. You'll be happy to know you won't be so horribly bored from now on. You're going to have company."

He looked to the empty bed by the window. "Nuts."

"I thought you'd be pleased. Someone to talk to."

"Probably an old man who's just had his gallbladder ripped out, or his kidneys reprocessed."

"No," she said, and seemed to think twice before finishing. "As a matter of fact, it's a kid."

"A what?"

"A kid. From the upstairs ward. There's been . . ." She smiled and shrugged. "He'll be down later. I'll be back to see how you guys get along."

"Thanks," he said sourly. "I know one lousy fairy tale, I don't like sports, and I haven't the slightest idea who has the number one record, country or rock. Wonderful."

"Sports?" she said. "You don't like sports?"

He looked mournfully at his leg, cleanly broken

in two places, the other one with calf muscles nearly torn to shreds. "Not anymore."

She laughed, and surprised him by blowing him a kiss. He tried to lean forward to watch her progress down the hall, but she was gone in an eye's blink, and he lay back, smiling.

It was a cliché, he supposed, that patients fall in love with either their doctors or their nurses, and once the hospital stay is over, they drift apart, shadows swallowed by the night; but in this case he had a feeling he was putting the lie to the saw. He didn't love Janey, he adored her; he waited impatiently for each visit on her rounds—for the beginning of each shift when she came to kiss him good morning, for the end of the shift when she kissed him goodnight. He fantasized how they might make love with him trussed and cast; he fantasized taking her home when he was better and showing her how he could make her a hell of a lot happier than she was right now.

Especially since, behind that smile, behind the wide blue eyes, he could see the apprehension.

They were all that way these past few days. The halls were less filled with chatter; the rattle and clatter of supply carts muffled and less hurried. Even the announcements over the PA system seemed more subdued.

He hadn't noticed it at first. He had been too

busy fighting through the drugs in his system, struggling out of postoperative recovery to feel the dull and constant throbbing in his newly set leg, the knife jabs that made him pray for a cast on the right one as well.

He was no hero, never wanted to be one; stoics were people who needed very long vacations. So he took every drop of medicine they prescribed for him, and the sleeping pills that seldom worked because he couldn't lie on his back, and he had to. For the first time in years he wept—at the pain, and the helplessness he couldn't relieve. The fall, and the snap of his bones, had terrified him, but only when he had realized what had happened; then he was furious at himself for being so stupid. For walking up to the Jasper house as if he were the police and had every right. The butler had opened the door, saw him on the porch and glared. Michael introduced himself. The butler turned away and a new man took his place. A large man. A very large man with hate in his eyes and damned strong hands that had picked him up and tossed him over the railing.

There were shrubs, but he'd missed them, pinwheeling in midair and landing just wrong.

He winced at the memory—of the flight and the fall.

It was stupid, incredibly stupid, and he should

have known those people would be touchy about reporters, but here in the hospital, listening to the quiet nightsounds, the whispers, smelling the anti-septic and hearing footfalls without seeing who was coming to his door . . .

It was only a broken leg, but it made him think of dying.

On the third day he felt fine, except for a little discomfort under the cast; over the fourth and fifth days he managed to find the right position to sleep in, the right way to sit so he could read the morn-ing paper, the proper way to behave when they gave him the bedpans. And once he had estab-lished a routine, and knew approximately when he was going to leave, the boredom set in. Had he been buried in work from the office, or had family in to see him every day, the tension among the staff might have swept right past him.

But he had been bored. So he listened, eaves-dropped, and knew why Janey had stopped herself before telling him there was trouble with the children.

As far as he could make out, one was dead, and one was missing, and she wouldn't tell him why.

Now he was going to get one of them in here with him. Just what he needed—an hysterical brat to keep calm while he was losing his mind.

Five minutes later the doctor walked in, looked

at him from the foot of the bed, clucked at his sour expression, and walked to his side to plant a kiss on his cheek.

"You'll scare the little bugger to death looking like that," she said, pushing long black hair away from her eyes. "Can't you at least smile?"

He did, stiffly, and she slapped his shoulder playfully, took his chart from the footboard and flipped it open. As he watched, he felt himself calming, thinking that a man who could be in love with two women at the same time can't be all that close to the lip of the grave. He might, he admitted when she pulled back his sheet and examined his right leg, be a little crazy and asking for trouble, but how could he not fall for a woman like this? Tall and slender, her profile sharp and soft at the same time, her hands so gentle, and her manner as well. He didn't think Janey would be jealous; she was the understanding type, and he doubted she would mind if some of his affection were shared.

"Well?"

"Hurts, right?"

"Carolyn, for god's sake."

"But not as bad as last week."

Grudgingly, he nodded.

"Good. Tomorrow you'll go upstairs and get a walking cast and be up on crutches for a little while. Practice for when you go home."

"Thank god for that," he said, and looked earnestly at the narrow door to the television's left. "No more bedpans, just lovely cold porcelain."

She laughed, patted his arm, and told him she'd be back to see him before she left for home. He couldn't persuade her to visit for a while longer, and sighed loudly when she left him, clasped his hands on his chest, and looked back at the ceiling.

Michael, he thought, you are a goddamned fool.

Which wouldn't be the first time, he reminded himself as he turned his head toward the window. Being a fool was what had cost him his last job, and he had been determined not to ruin his chances here, in Oxrun Station. He was not going to let an old friend down, especially when that old friend had thrown him a lifeline.

"All you have to do," Marc Clayton had told him, "is go out to the Jasper place on the Pike. I haven't heard anything from the police, but maybe you can convince the old man that we can help him. At least find out if there's been a ransom note, or a call. Just be cool, Mike, be cool. This isn't Boston; this is the Station. It wouldn't hurt to be low-key."

He never had the chance, and now Marc was calling him once a day or so, half laughing at the episode, half reminding him he was still on salary and whatever had happened to the Jasper family wouldn't go away just because he was resting.

"Resting? You call this resting, you—"

"Just keep in touch, pal. You haven't broken your dialing finger yet."

He shifted, froze when he expected his legs to protest, then relaxed and watched the pine trees through the window. There was a wind, and their tops swayed, whipping in the gusts and settling again. It was hypnotic, and he started to doze, shook out of it with a grunt when he sensed someone standing in the doorway.

It was a young woman.

"Hi," she said. "I'm Cora. Mr. Clayton sent me, to help you out if I can."

Then she moved into the room hastily with a muttered apology left behind her, and Michael saw the wheelchair, Janey, and eventually, the boy.

There was a great deal of confusion as the nurse and Cora did a dance to avoid collision, and Carolyn marched through with orders for moving in. Michael watched it all with amusement, deciding on the spot it wouldn't hurt to love three women, not if they were realistic about a man crippled in his bed and his emotions in turmoil. He almost forgot about the boy until he heard the bed squeaking on the other side of the curtain Janey had pulled along its ceiling track. Shadows swayed, swelled, and shrank, and he looked away from it with a shudder; it was too much like the nightmares he'd had when he was little—things that prowled, things that stalked, things that came to him in shadows on his nursery wall.

It was silly. It was the remnants of the drugs. It was all he could do to put a smile on his face when the curtain was drawn back, and the three women were ranged around the young boy's bed. Nine, perhaps ten, with red hair and freckles and a large padded bandage that covered his left ear. He wasn't smiling, and finally Carolyn ushered the others out, returned, and stood between the two beds.

"Mr. Kolle," she said with a nod to Michael, "I'd like you to meet Mr. Rory Castle. Mr. Castle has had his appendix out. He will also probably talk your ear off."

She blew a kiss to both of them, left with white coat flapping, and Michael cleared his throat.

"I didn't know you had to stay in so long for something like that."

Rory sat up, pushed away the sheets, and crossed his legs. "I had . . ." He touched the bandaged ear. "I don't know. They told my mom all about it, but they didn't tell me."

"Complications?"

The boy nodded. "Yeah, that's it! Something happened, and they had to fix my ear, too."

"Is Miss Player your doctor?"

"Yep. Neat, ain't she?"

Yeah, he thought; neat is right.

"Wow!" Rory moved closer to the edge of his bed. "How'd you do that?"

"Fell off a porch."

"Wow. Wow, that's neat."

"You think so, huh?"

"Yeah," the boy said. "It looks better than this stupid thing on my head."

They talked for the next hour, Rory's eyes widening when he learned Michael was a reporter, shifting away when he was asked if other kids had been moved. They were, but he wouldn't talk about them, and Michael decided not to push it just yet. It occurred to him that he had been handed a byline on a silver platter, and all he had to do was make friends with Freckles.

And that, he soon realized, wouldn't be hard.

Carolyn was right—the boy talked as if he'd been locked away for most of his life. He talked about his schoolmates, his teachers, his pets, his house, and when all that was done, he began to tell stories. All kinds of stories. About cowboys, and cops and robbers, and spaceships, and sports, not once finishing one, something he'd said reminding him of something else and sending him off on an entirely new tale. Michael listened, and nodded, and laughed when he was supposed to, and didn't feel at all guilty when he finally shouted, ''Enough, boy, for god's sake. Have pity on an old man.''

''But you're not old,'' Rory said.

''I will be if you keep it up. Old before my time and collecting my pension.''

Rory wanted to know what a pension was.

He told him they were both too young, and maybe it would be a good idea if they both rested a while.

Rory laughed, and started a story about his grandfather that made Michael groan; and it wasn't until dinner that he remembered the girl, Cora, and realized it was too late to call Marc and find out what was going on. He didn't object to the help, but he would have thought Clayton would have given him some warning. For a moment he wondered if the woman's appearance was a comment on his abilities, and once the moment had passed, he knew he was being childish. Feeling sorry for himself again, when he ought to be thinking of ways to use her as his eyes, as well as his legs.

He grunted, swore, and blinked when the boy giggled. He'd forgotten all about Freckles and would have to get used to keeping his comments to himself.

He ate then and traded acid reviews of the meal with Rory and the orderly who took the trays away. The boy, he noticed, had eaten very little, and when the television was turned on, Mike spent as much time watching him as he did the small screen. Rory had grown silent, nervous, his hands clutching the sheets into clumps, smoothing them out, clutching them again. He looked to the door several times, to the window, which reflected nothing but the room.

And the only thing he said before the lights were turned out was, "Mr. Kolle, do you ever have nightmares?"

At night. All night. The hospital whispering to itself in faint footsteps along the hall, the wind testing the windows, every so often a low moan from another room, a muffled chime, a hiss-and-delayed thud as elevator doors opened and shut and no one came out, no one went in.

All night. Bedsprings and sheets and the scratch of a pencil, the burr of a telephone, somewhere down around the corner a toilet flushing and the scuff of worn slippers and the flaplike wings of a nightgown on thin legs.

All night.

Without dreams.

Feeling like a child who couldn't call his mother.

*   *   *

When he woke in the morning, Michael felt as if he hadn't slept a wink. His eyes stung and his bladder was swollen, and when he saw the crutches leaning against the wall beside his head, he knew he didn't want to use the bedpan again. Slowly, exaggerating every movement in case he was ambushed with pain, he swung both legs over the side of the mattress and sat there, head down, breathing steadily and grinning because he was so proud for not killing himself.

He reached for his crutches.

He saw Rory watching him, and swore him to secrecy with a raised fist and a scowl.

The boy grinned.

He set the padded tops under his arms and swayed to a standing, prayed, and moved across the floor. By the time he reached the bathroom door, his mending leg was screaming and his arms were cramping and his hands on the grips felt as if they were holding molten iron.

Rory applauded and giggled.

Michael closed the door, flipped the bowl's lid, and sat down, and sighed, glad for the first time he was wearing the standard gown that never shut in back, knowing the full meaning of heaven and vowing never again to take his plumbing for granted.

Janey found him in there, yelled without raising

her voice, and virtually dragged him back to bed. Didn't he know, she asked acidly, there were procedures to follow? Someone had to show him how to use the crutches so he wouldn't fall on his face and break his nose, so his legs would behave, so he could go a fair distance without dislocating a shoulder.

"I know, I know," he said, unable to stop grinning. "I didn't do so bad, though, all things considered."

"You were lucky."

"I am bored!"

She didn't kiss him, didn't tickle him, only told him to stop acting like a child, that she would make a full report of his behavior to Dr. Player.

"Boy," Rory said after she'd gone, "she's a grouch."

An orderly came in with a gurney. After a moment's sullen staring, Michael winked at Rory, climbed aboard, and was brought upstairs, where new X rays were taken and, an hour later, a shorter, sturdier walking cast was substituted for the one he already had. No one said a word to him; none even looked up when he asked about the children.

When Carolyn finally arrived on her rounds, she was cool, distant, mechanically going through the instructions of using new cast and crutches and telling him he had to practice once every hour until the middle of the afternoon. The leg would hurt like hell; he wasn't to let it bother him. The more he moved around, the more used to it he'd get.

He didn't know why, but he couldn't help feeling she was stalling, and didn't mention the lines that were deep by her eyes, the weariness that drew down the hard corners of her mouth.

"Jeez," Rory said when she'd finished checking his ear and his side, "you're sure grumpy."

She glared at him, glared at Michael, and marched out of the room.

"What did I say?" the boy asked.

"Nothing," Michael assured him. "I guess today just isn't a good day all the way around."

"Nuts," the boy said and stared glumly at the wall.

Shortly afterward, Rory was sent off in a wheelchair to see his parents in the visitors' room, and Michael got on the crutches again and practiced as he was told. Every hour. Once an hour. Damning the cast for being so damned heavy. Damning his good leg for being so damned weak. He didn't fall, though he came close twice, and once lunch had been cleared away and the throbbing had eased, he decided to take the measure of the hall.

"I don't think Dr. Player's gonna like that," Rory warned when he returned.

Michael grinned at him. "The way she's feeling today, if I dropped dead, she'd sue me. What have I got to lose?"

"She could lock you up, put you in solitary."

"Not me, pal. She loves me, you know."

Rory made a face, and he threatened him with a sound thrashing, laughing until he saw the panicked look on the boy's face.

Shit, he thought; Kolle, you've got a lot to learn about handling kids.

He waited until he was sure Rory knew he was kidding, then leaned against the jamb and checked for a destination, a goal he had to reach before he dropped of exhaustion.

The easiest way would be straight ahead, along the white and soft-brown tiled corridor that split the building in half. But if he went there, he would have to pass two pairs of elevators facing each other, examination and storage rooms, and the nurses' station. That was too many people he might meet and who might see him fall, too many nurses who might question his journey.

Left would take him to the rear of the building and the intensive care units; the opposite way would bring him to the front and, at the corner, a large open area—a visitors' room, where patients sat with their families, had coffee and snacks from machines, and watched the trees and sky through dark-tinted windows that reached to the ceiling.

He liked the idea of coffee not brewed in the hospital's miserable excuse for a kitchen. On the other hand, he didn't want all those people laughing at him should he slip. Damn, he thought, closed his eyes, and flipped a coin. A slow inhalation, and he swung to the right, keeping close to the wall and avoiding nosey stares into the other patients' rooms ranged along the hospital's outer rim.

He half expected, half hoped for, Carolyn or Janey to show up and scold him for his foolishness, then drag him back where he belonged. When nothing happened, he hobbled on, ignoring his left leg while he found the rhythm that matched the weight of his cast and the swing of the crutches. It wasn't fun, but it was mobility, and by the time he reached the visiting room, he was sweating and feeling just fine.

And then, not so fine at all.

The room was twenty feet long, almost that wide, and the light through all the windows turned suddenly bright. White. Brilliant white. Bleaching the walls, shifting the molded plastic chairs and long plastic tables to sharp-edged black stone. He squinted as he passed over a metal floor strip that guided shut sliding doors when visiting hours were over, and hesitated when he realized no one was here. He groped for the nearest chair, couldn't find one, and swung around on his crutches to face the way he had come.

"Jesus," he muttered.

White. Blinding white filling the window at the hall's far end, spilling from the rooms and covering the floor, killing shadows and colors, bringing tears to his eyes, and stoppering his ears as if he were deaf.

He felt himself swaying but there was nothing to hold on to, and he cursed his stubborn pride, cursed the doctors and nurses, cursed the burning pain that spiraled beneath the cast and made him grip the crutches so tightly he could feel his fingers beginning to cramp.

Something touched him behind his knees.

Someone's hand dropped lightly to his shoulder.

Someone said, "Sit," and he didn't question the order. He lowered himself into a wheelchair, gathered the crutches between his legs, and felt his leg tremble as it held the cast an inch off the floor.

"Thanks," he said. "God, I thought I was going to die."

"You're not going to die, don't worry about it."

They turned right, into the light, and he lowered his head to keep the tears from returning.

"No offense, but this isn't the way to my room."

"I know. I just thought you'd like a tour or something."

He looked up and over his shoulder, but the damned light had turned the woman's face to shadow. "Cora?"

"Yeah. Hi, Mr. Kolle!" Brightly. Smiling, though he couldn't see it. "How are you doing?" A high-pitched laugh, a young girl's laugh, and the wheelchair swerved when she covered her mouth.

He looked straight ahead, shading his eyes, wondering what the hell was going on outside. Cora said she didn't know, probably just a break in the clouds.

"What clouds?"

"What clouds? It's been raining all morning."

How nice, he thought, angry that he hadn't even noticed the damned weather.

"Mr. Clayton," she said a few yards later, "wants me to tell you everything's okay on the insurance. If they try to charge you for something, sue them."

One of the wheels needed oiling. He shifted the crutches until they were lying across the armrests. It didn't matter. No one was in the hall but them it seemed.

She talked rapidly, almost nervously, telling him

about the weather, the work on Centre Street that was replacing blacktop with brick, the way the boy with the bandaged ear wouldn't talk to her even though she'd brought him some candy.

"Rory," he said. "His name is Rory."

"Weird."

"Scared, Cora."

They paused at the corner, swung left, and moved on, through the light, soft and soothing, turning the few passersby into silent, nunlike shadows that were swallowed again as soon as they moved on.

He was reminded of cloisters and didn't know why.

"Scared? No kidding. Of what?"

"I don't know. That's why you're going to help me."

She leaned down, her lips close to his right ear. "Me?"

"Well, sure. Aren't you supposed to be my legs?"

"Oh. Right."

They passed the middle corridor, and he heard an elevator's door hiss open, hiss shut. No footsteps. No gurneys. No chatter at the nurses' station.

The medicine, he thought then. His stomach churned briefly; he swallowed bile and took a breath.

"What do you want me to do?"

He started, not realizing he had almost dozed off, and had to think a moment to remember what she was talking about. "The children's ward is where, upstairs?"

"Down," she said. "In back. Upstairs are the operating rooms and the labs, stuff like that."

"So go downstairs," he said. "Talk to the nurses. Find a doctor and talk to him. See why they're moving the kids out."

When she didn't answer right away, he thought she hadn't been listening; then she grunted, and moved a little faster. On the left were windows, most of them blanked by white blinds, the dying behind them and "No Smoking" on the doors.

"Mr. Kolle?" Whispering now, as if in deference to the place, and to the silence it commanded.

"What?"

"Why'd you come to the Station?"

Mike, his former editor had said, *you do not walk up to the mayor of Boston, shove a pad and pen in his face, and ask him flat out if he knew, when he bought that harbor-front parcel, that they were going to kick out the lobstermen and bring in the condos.*

"I didn't much like the city."

You're too eager, Mike. You gotta be patient when you're fishing for the big ones.

"You like this place better? Really?"

241

Patience, he had thought, was for cowards, and for people who had buckled to the weight of the system; patience, he discovered, was the hardest thing to learn.

"I like it okay."

Around the corner, toward his own room, the light fading, colors returning, noises once again unmuffled and sharp.

Cora wheeled him in, careful of his extended leg, and he saw that Rory was gone, his bed still unmade. She said something about the kid going for an ear test or exam, helped him onto the mattress, and put the chair beside the window. Then she reached down by the door and with a smile held up a large white wicker basket filled with fruit and cheese, covered with cellophane she tore off with a flourish.

"From the office," she said. Smiled shyly. "And me. I know what it's like to be stuck in a place like this. It's awful. The pits."

She was, he saw now, much younger than he'd first thought. Barely out of her twenties, rather pale, and too slender. She looked ill and too proud to give in to it; she looked, he thought, as if she were dying.

"Cora, you all right?" Fussing with his bathrobe, holding his leg above the cast to subdue the pain.

Startled, she tried a smile. "I'm tired, that's all. Mr. Clayton's a real slave driver. He says, if I want to learn the business, I have to learn all of it, even back where they print it. I told him I just wanted to learn investigative reporting, and he said that was redundant." A melancholy frown as she placed the basket on the table. "I don't think I'm gonna stick around very long."

"You could learn from worse," he said. "Marc Clayton's a hell of a man."

Working five years for the *Globe*, from the time of his graduation, wanting it all before he was thirty, before he was too old to enjoy it. Running around like a jackass, hunting the elusive scoop that would bring him his fame, his fortune, his gold-plated place in the journalistic sun.

Playing at Clark Kent without the costume underneath.

Christ, he thought when he looked at the girl; Christ.

Music from the next room until a nurse turned it down; an orderly shambling behind a broom and a bow wave of dust.

"Hey," she said suddenly, and pushed a hand through her hair. "If I'm gonna get what you want, I'd better move it, huh?" She reached into the basket and grabbed an apple, shined it on her breast and kissed it, and winked. "I picked this one myself,'' she said as she tossed it into his lap. ''I didn't think you wanted all that garbage they spray on them in the store, y'know? They even have artificial coloring, for god's sake.''

He didn't wince when it landed on his groin, didn't say anything about organic versus cheap. He only picked it up, saw himself in the red that was deeper than a mirror, and winked back as he took a bite.

''Pretty good, huh? An apple a day, right?''

''I should have had one before.'' She looked away, and he raised an eyebrow. ''You have trees in your backyard?''

It was sweet, juicy, with a slight afterbite.

She grinned and walked to the door. ''Are you kidding? My father can barely grow grass. No, it's from the orchard. You know it, on the other side of Mainland?''

He thought, and shook his head. ''I'm still new, I guess.''

''That's all right. I only found out about it when my sister dragged me on this really gross picnic last spring. Jesus.'' Her mouth twisted in disgust. ''Kids, you know what I mean?''

''Yeah,'' he said solemnly. ''Pains in the ass.''

A laugh, a blown kiss from her palm, and she cautioned him not to eat it too fast. With the food he was getting now, he'd probably throw it up.

Then she was gone, and he lay there with the bed cranked up and the bed beside him empty and the apple turning warm as he turned it over in his hand.

He slept, woke just before dinner, and jumped when he saw someone standing beside him. It was Rory, huddling in his bathrobe, and he'd been crying.

Michael repositioned the bed up so he could sit without strangling, realized he still had the apple in his hand, and laid it on the table.

"Mr. Kolle?" the boy said, wiping a sleeve under his nose. "Mr. Kolle, I want to go home."

He didn't know what to say, and couldn't say a thing when the orderly wheeled in the supper cart, cheerfully spreading the good word from the gloomy outside, hustling Rory to his bed, and serving the trays with a flourish. After he left, they ate in silence, and when the remains were taken away, he didn't object when Rory, with a pleading look, climbed onto the bed beside him, shivering, his freckles so dark against the pale white of his face they made his cheeks hollow, his nose too sharp.

"I hate hospitals too," he said softly.

Rory nodded, curled up, and snuggled against his side. When he looked down, he saw the boy with a thumb in his mouth.

The window was dark, and in the panes a wavering reflection of the floor's central hall. A ghost at the nurses' station, ghosts leaving the elevator, no Janey, no Carolyn, and he wondered what was wrong.

Rory shifted, and he felt awkward, not knowing whether to stroke his hair, his back, say anything more and try to make a joke about the horrors of temporary living in a place that only knew your name by the chart on your bed. But it was more, he suspected, than not being able to play with his friends.

"Did you see what happened?" he asked after a while, looking to the open door, looking up the hall at the white-dressed traffic that passed the room in silence.

Rory shook his head.

"Did the police come?"

The boy shook his head again.

"Just a bunch of doctors and things, huh?"

Rory nodded once, his forehead thumping Michael's ribs.

"I'll bet," he said after a few minutes more, "it was a kind of sickness. I mean, sometimes kids get things that spread real fast, like measles and stuff. Some little dope brings it in from the outside and the next thing you know a zillion people are walking around with red spots all over their faces. It happens. So they move the other kids out for a while, until everyone is better."

"Really?"

"Would I lie to you, kid?"

And when he looked down, the boy was shaking his head, wanting and not knowing how to tell him he was wrong.

"Thank you."

Michael turned his head and saw Carolyn at the door. "Thanks for what?"

"For helping," she said, coming in, nodding to Rory as she looked at his chart. "A hospital is bad enough for a kid without crap like this." She was annoyed, almost mad, but she made an effort to be friendly as she examined the cast, eyed the crutches with a faint frown, then moved Rory to his own bed with a promise he could return. "These," she said then, pointing at the bandages, "can go."

"Thank god. Will I be able to play the violin?"

She unwrapped the leg, tossed the soiled bandages into the trash can, wrinkled her nose, and straightened. "God, you could use a bath, Mike."

"Ready when you are," he said.

The leg was crossed with scabbed scratches, and a large yellowed bruise spread from his knee to his instep. He almost gagged when he saw it, and when he reached down, it was tender, the odor like something he would expect to find in the morgue.

"I'll have someone come in," she told him,

pushed him flat with the flat of her hand, and listened to his heart, took his pulse, checked his eyes with a light that reminded him of that afternoon. When she was finished, she scribbled something on the chart and looked at his face.

"I'm sorry," she said quietly. "I didn't mean to snap at you before."

"My fault. I'm . . ." He shrugged. "I hate being cooped up, helpless, you know?"

She kissed his forehead, brushed a finger over his lips, and he watched as she attended to Rory, tickling him, mussing his hair because she knew how much he disliked it, finally telling him not to pay any attention to what the ape in the other bed said because he's only a reporter, and everyone knows that reporters have to take a college course in advanced lying before they get their diplomas.

"Hey!" he protested.

Rory looked around her arm and grinned.

"Doc, that's slander."

She rose and smiled without showing her teeth. "Sue me."

He appealed to the boy, who was trying not to laugh, then widened his eyes when Carolyn left and Janey came in, pushing a cart in front of her with a large chrome bowl filled with steaming water. "What the hell is that?"

"Your bath, sir," she said. And looked at Rory. "You want to help me scald him to death?"

It was the best five minutes he'd spent since he'd arrived—Rory kneeling on the bed, giggling and holding his arms down while Janey scrubbed his leg, swearing at the bits of adhesive that wouldn't come off, comparing the smell of his wizened flesh to charnel houses she had known. He complained, he threatened, he told Rory he would pluck his freckles off one by one if he didn't let go.

Rory laughed.

Janey laughed.

And he played the martyr as well as he could until in his feigned tossing he saw the dark window.

There was something out there looking in.

Bending his right arm to bring Rory over his chest, he stared and realized it was only a reflection. A figure in the hall just out of the elevator, looking down to his room, darker than the night that framed it, larger than it should have been, and vanishing as soon as a nurse with a bedpan approached it, walked through it.

"There!" Janey said, slapping his knee hard. "You are now almost civilized." And exchanged glances with Rory when she saw he wasn't paying attention. "Hey, Mike, I'm done."

Rory looked at the window, and scrambled off to his own bed.

Janey looked at the window, back to Mike, and adjusted her cap. "It's dark out, you know. You can't see anything."

"Yeah," he said. "I was just looking, that's all."

She gathered washcloths and towels, told him not to walk too much—she had heard of his around-the-world trip this afternoon and didn't think it was a good idea to practice every day—and she'd be back in the morning.

She kissed him lightly.

He didn't kiss her back. The affection in her touch wasn't anything like the blank look in her eyes.

Then Rory's parents came for a visit, and he was left alone, finally wishing he had gotten Cora's home number so he could find out what she had learned from the ward downstairs. If anything, he thought sourly. She probably just flirted with an intern, was intimidated by the head nurse, and decided on her own there wasn't anything there. Which meant, if he was right, he would have to do it on his own.

He tried calling Marc, but no one was home.

He tried calling Chief Stockton to see if anyone had demanded ransom for the missing Jasper boy, and was told that the chief and the detectives on the case weren't giving out information, at the family's request.

By the time he was finished, four fruitless calls later, he was angry and ready to pack his crutches and leave. It was dumb. It was stupid. How the hell did Marc expect him to work when he was tied down like this? And how the hell, he asked himself, did he expect to get anything done now, at night, when he'd done nothing that afternoon but play hero in crutches?

That one was easy—he was afraid. He was creating obstacles where none existed because he didn't want to know if, in all his years of learning, he had learned anything at all.

Listen, Marc had said, *you should know all this stuff already. You don't belong here, you belong back in Boston.*

What he didn't say was obvious—*as soon as you grow up and stop running.*

The leg under the cast began itching, and he squirmed, reached down, and wasn't surprised when his fingers were just too short to reach far enough under the cast. He drummed. He gritted his teeth. He hummed a prayer for a miracle to banish the torment. Then he grabbed for his crutches and hauled himself off the bed.

"I thought you were supposed to stay there."

He spun and nearly fell, gaping until he recognized Rory lying in his bed. "Jesus, I didn't know you were back."

"My mom says I'm as quiet as a mouse. Where are you going?"

He pointed to the cast. "It itches. I am going to hold a nurse hostage until they get me something I can stick down there. Then I'm going to scratch like crazy."

The boy should have laughed, he thought; at least a smile. But he lay there, bathrobe still on, arms down at his sides and fingers grabbing the sheet, his bandaged ear looking twice as large as when he'd left.

"See you in a little while."

Rory blinked for a nod.

And as he stepped out into the hall, he heard: "Mr. Kolle, where do monsters come from?"

He made it to the nurses' station without falling, testing his newly unbandaged leg and finding it wobbly but reasonably strong. Then he begged the woman on duty to demolish a coat hanger he saw on the desk behind her. She laughed and deftly twisted the wire into something he could use, laughed again when he instantly shoved it into his cast and probed until he found the right place. He worked at it slowly, not wanting to break the skin, and sighed loudly when at last he pronounced himself cured.

The woman shook her head and ordered him politely back to his room.

He bowed as best he could, gripped the hanger in his teeth, and turned around with a brisk salute. Then he turned back and asked how the children were doing, if everything was okay downstairs in the ward.

She stared at him blankly. "What children?" she said.

He lifted a hand to point, grabbed the crutch quickly when he felt himself tipping, and shrugged. "Nothing," he said, tasting the hanger as his tongue flicked against it. "Don't listen to me, I'm hysterical."

She sighed and ordered him away again.

He considered arguing. Someone else on the floor might know what he was talking about, but she was losing patience and good humor, and he decided not to press his luck. A nod, then, a farewell smile, and he steadied himself for the trip home. His foot slipped on the knob at the bottom of the walking cast, and by the time he had righted himself, sweating, cursing, he saw Rory in the doorway, arms tight across his chest and his hair in disarray.

"Hey," he called out. "Hang on, kiddo. I'll be there in a minute. Long John Silver to the rescue, what do you think?"

Rory ducked back into the room with a quick shake of his head.

A look to the nurse and a shrug, and he thumped his way past the elevators, glancing at the unlit numbers over the doors, remembering the figure he'd seen, and not seen, here last night. Much more of that, he thought, and they'd be putting him in the psycho ward, brilliant reporter or not.

At the T-intersection he paused and leaned against the wall. A glance to his left at the visiting room showed him it was empty; to the right, and the window at the end of the hall was blacker, for the dim lights recessed in the ceiling. Then he looked straight ahead, into his room, and saw Rory sitting in the wheelchair. Staring out. Not moving.

Hobbling to the door, he tilted his head side to side to display the hanger in his teeth and deliberately mumbled something he knew the boy wouldn't understand.

Rory didn't move.

"Hey, pal," he said gently. "What's up?"

"The monsters," the boy whispered.

Michael couldn't help it; he looked over his shoulder.

There was no one in the hall.

He spat the hanger out, grimaced at the taste still lingering in his mouth, and sat on the edge of his bed, beckoning until the boy wheeled himself over.

"Now what's all this about monsters?" he said,

trying to remain as serious as Rory looked. "Am I in for another one of your crazy stories?"

The boy shook his head, wouldn't look up. "Where do they come from?" A small voice, a night voice just out of a nightmare.

Michael shifted awkwardly until he could swing his cast onto the mattress, foot on the pillow, and tuck his other leg underneath. Resting on his elbow then, he was near to eye level and tried not to listen to the silence he heard.

"In here," he said, tapping a finger to his forehead.

Rory blinked. "I don't think so."

"Sure they do, pal. You know what imagination is, right? God, you ought to, with all that stuff you've been handing out."

Rory nodded, reluctantly, his eyes half closed as if fighting a headache.

"Well, that's where they come from. Your imagination. Some guy, see, gets scared of a shadow and they turn it into some really creepy thing that hides under the bed, or in the closet, or under the porch. But it isn't real because you made it up. So you stick your tongue out at it and it goes away. Or you turn on the light. Something like that."

Again the child's voice: "Are you sure?"

He looked around the room, wishing the kid's parents would magically pop out of the bathroom and explain how to deal with something like this. Of course he was sure, but how do you explain it to someone who believes?

"Yes," he said firmly. "Imagination is what makes movies and books and comics and television shows. It's what makes my job, sometimes, when I have to imagine what this guy or that guy was thinking when he did something. It helps to clear away all the garbage and get me what I want." Easy, he thought then; easy, you're lecturing. "See, I have to look for facts, Rory. And sometimes my imagination helps me find them."

"Don't . . . don't you ever get in trouble?"

He laughed, knowing the boy would never understand. "You, my friend, have just hit the nail right on the head. Trouble? I have been in such trouble, you wouldn't believe it." He leaned forward and reached out to tap the boy's knee. "And you know why I got into trouble, my boy? Because I let my imagination run away with me."

Rory looked to his pillow, looked at Michael sideways, and wheeled the chair back to the window. He got up, took off his robe, and climbed into bed, pulling the thin blanket up to his chin. "The monsters?"

"You mean the ones downstairs or—"

"Yes."

"Imagination."

Rory put a hand on his bandage, winced, and nodded.

Michael waited, then maneuvered himself under his own covers, sitting under the tiny light that barely reached to his feet. The rest of the room was dark. He could hear Rory breathing, every so often shifting his legs across the sheets.

"Hey, pal?"

"What?"

Michael sat up to see over the bedtable. "Where did you see these monsters of yours?"

There was no response for several seconds, and Michael thought he'd fallen asleep. Then he pulled one arm from under the blanket and pointed to the floor.

All night.

Whispering.

And the shadows of dreams.

The next morning Michael screamed.

The moment he opened his eyes it was there, working out of his throat from the fire rushing through his legs, from the burning on his palms, from the bars that had been thrust through one shoulder to the other. The effort to keep silent spun the scream into a groan, and he grabbed for the call button on the wire by his head.

Holding himself rigid. Keeping his eyes closed. Nodding when he heard Janey asking sadly about the pain.

"You're just a big kid, you know that, Mike?"

Janey. Lovely Janey.

"Now be a good boy and wait, and I'll see if Doctor Player will let you have something to take care of it."

Shit on growing up, he thought, if it means I can't cry.

"Janey?"

Slipping a hand behind his head a few minutes later, holding a paper cup to his lips, putting a pill on his tongue, waiting while she stroked his chest until the medicine was down. Whispering something in his ear and kissing his cheek, shifting and drawing the curtain around him.

Drifting.

Dozing.

Waking sometime past noon to see a pair of white coats standing by Rory's empty bed, looking at the boy's chart, looking up at him and telling him with their eyes he'd best rest, go back to sleep. Carolyn bent over him, brushed back his hair, and whispered something in his ear.

"Carolyn?"

"Hush. Go to sleep."

"Carolyn, my head hurts."

"It's all right. When you wake up, everything will be fine."

Drifting.

Dozing.

The telephone waking him, the ringing cut off before he could reach the receiver. Turning his head, seeing Rory motionless, asleep, a fresh bandage now covering half his skull along the left side, wisps and ferns of red hair poking into the air.

Story, he thought as he drifted off again; story, there's a story, but he couldn't open his mouth.

Waking a third time to damn his impatience. If he hadn't been so anxious to walk a hundred miles the day before, he wouldn't be stuck now, gripping his right thigh to corral the pain below his waist, taking deep breaths as the medicine played with his vision and filled his mouth with damp cotton.

"Hey, Rory, am I dead or what?" he said with a laugh when the pain subsided and he could think again. "God, I think I could drink a ton of water without even floating."

There was no answer.

"Y'know, it feels like someone put dynamite in my head. I think if I sneeze, I'm gonna blow my brains out."

Still no answer, and he passed a hand over his

face, over his chest, and realized that the room was in twilight, the door partially closed. The sun was gone, the blinds drawn to the sill, and little more than a lighter dark slipped in from the hall.

Swallowing, he looked over to see if the boy was asleep; rubbing his eyes, he pushed up on his elbows.

The bed was empty, sheets and pillow gone, blanket folded at the foot. The chart wasn't on its hook.

A sympathetic sigh no one heard. The boy hadn't gone home; they must have moved him again. And from the way whatever was wrong with his ear was progressing, it was probably into a private room on the building's other side, or down to intensive care, where he could be monitored more closely.

He shook his head slowly, and regretted it immediately when the headache flared and made him gasp, and sent orange pinwheels through his eyes.

"Oh, brother," he gasped. "Oh, god, where's the aspirin?"

Not moving until it passed, looking again at Rory's bed and hating to think of the kid with tubes and wires and all those freckles fading to nothing. That sort of thing wasn't fair, not when you were just a boy and couldn't protect yourself.

His stomach growled. Mindful of the explosion

he could bring on if he moved fast, he reached for the basket of fruit Cora had brought, and yanked his hand back. It was empty, and the apple he'd taken the bite from was still on the table, shriveled and brown, with a fly walking on its skin.

Jesus, he thought, grimacing in distaste and working his arms until he was upright. He reached down to his left and picked up the small trash can, held it against the table, and brushed the apple off, and the basket. Voracious orderlies, he decided, or a nurse, maybe Rory's parents or doctors. It didn't make any difference; he was still hungry, and he used the call button in hopes he could wheedle some food from the night shift.

A minute later he tried again.

A minute after that he threw the covers aside and reached for his crutches. He had to use the bathroom anyway, and while he was up he could look into the hall and maybe flag someone down.

His legs wobbled and held him, the headache didn't return but remained a distant throbbing, like the throbbing under the cast, and when he was at the door, feeling little better, he looked toward the nurses' station and saw it deserted. After a curse for rotten luck, he hopped backward on his good leg, perched on the metal footboard, and massaged his thighs. An emergency somewhere. He would have to wait and try again.

And as he did, he thought of Rory, wondering what it would be like to have a boy of his own. One to watch, to take care of, to lie to and tell stories to and mark his own years by the birthdays he had. How much of it was romance, and how much was plain work? He guessed that, with Rory, a lot of it was listening to tall tales and excuses and doing your best not to laugh when you were supposed to be angry.

He leaned forward, saw no one, and made his way to the bedtable, picked up the phone's receiver, and smiled when Marc answered, laughed when the editor demanded he stop goldbricking and get his ass back to work.

"But I have good news," Marc said. "The Jasper boy is back."

"What?"

"Right. They found him a few hours ago, up in Portland. Apparently the kidnappers got cold feet, jammed him in a sack, and dumped him in someone's backyard. He's okay, just scared as hell. Jasper's giving the family that found him something like fifteen grand and a new car."

"Damn," he said. "There goes my Pulitzer."

Feeling the first sting of another headache, and looking over his shoulder when he heard a scratching in the hall.

"Mike, I have an idea. It won't be a Pulitzer,

but it might do you some good. Just hear me out before you say yes or no, and don't jump to conclusions.''

A distant scratching, a nail drawn along the floor from the bottom of an old push broom, a child walking with a stick he held to the wall.

Michael pulled the receiver away from his ear, listened harder, leaned back in order to peer through the door.

Marc kept on talking, almost urgently now.

The scratching, louder. And no one complaining.

''Damnit, Mike, are you listening to me?''

The scratching stopped.

Making faces and rubbing his temples as the headache grew stronger.

''Kolle, are you there?''

Footsteps now, from the other direction, heavy and uneven, a man on a bad leg, or a man on a false one. Step-tap, a deep breath; step-tap, and a sigh.

''Michael!''

''I'm here, I'm here,'' he said, cupping his hand around the mouthpiece, staring at the door.

''Well, did you hear anything I said?''

Step-tap, a deep breath; step-tap, and a moan.

''Jesus Christ,'' Michael whispered.

''Mike, what the hell's going on?'' Clayton demanded. "Did they give you something? A sedative?"

"Marc, I need to get hold of Cora, okay? She didn't give me her home number and I need her here, now."

Step-tap, and silence.

The nightwind soughing in the pines.

He was watching a dim glow grow brighter up by the front of the building when something Clayton said made him turn from the door. "What? Say that again?" And he could hear strained patience in a long exhalation.

"I said, 'Cora who?' "

"Cora who? C'mon, Marc. Cora from the paper, the kid, who else?" The cord wrapped around a finger, the base sliding along the table. "She said . . . she told me you said she was supposed to work with me."

"Mike, I . . ." Clayton stopped and cleared his throat. "Mike, I don't have any Cora working for me. Never did."

"You're kidding."

The room brightened, whitely.

"In fact, the only Cora I know is Cora Keane."

"Then it must have been her."

"Not likely, Mike. She committed suicide after her sister disappeared."

"Now wait a minute," he said. "Wait a minute, let me get this straight. Are you telling me—''

The dial tone stopped him, and stopped completely when he tried to regain the connection. He didn't try a second time because the light grew even brighter, slamming shadows against the back wall, painting the window a dead black. The crutches felt chilled, but he flexed his fingers as he moved, to the end of the bed, to the edge of the door, looking out after swallowing and licking his lips, closing his eyes against the pain that swelled from his nape and filled his skull with a roaring.

Breathe, he ordered sternly; breathe, it'll pass.

And when it did, he looked out again.

There was no one to his left, no one to his right, everything touched and washed by the same sourceless white.

He told himself not to worry, that something was wrong with the power, like bulbs that flare up just before they blow out, and all he had to do was sit down and wait and someone would be around to let him know what was going on.

An elevator opened.

A dark figure stepped out, paused, and walked away.

He didn't bother to squint or shade his eyes because he recognized Janey immediately from her walk, the swing of her hips, the way her winged cap sat on her hair as if ready to fly away. Relieved and somewhat angry, he stumped out of the room and called her name, half turning his head against the glare and calling again when she ignored him. Stopping when she disappeared into the nurses' station, he heard something coming toward him, quickly on his right.

Step-tap, and sighing.

Black and still a part of the light, a fragment broken off and moving, the white glow around it as if turned to fog, forming, re-forming, erasing it and bringing it back, this time much smaller, and the step-tap was a padding, and the sighing was a growl.

He started to run and almost fell, blinked sweat from his eyes, and forced himself to use the gait of crutches and cast. Hitting the elevator call button as he passed, both up and down, then swinging into the station where Janey was sitting.

"You're supposed to be in bed," she said.

"Janey, what the . . ." He looked around in dumb amazement, looked back for an answer, and saw her roll the chair away from the report she was writing.

"Why aren't you in bed?" she asked, shaking a *naughty-boy* finger as though she were his mother.

"Janey, for god's sake, come on, huh?"

She rose and put her hands on her hips. "I won't tell you again, you hear? I've had enough."

It's all right, he thought, when he felt the fear touch him. It's all right; she's just tired and you're still a bit punchy.

"Janey—"

"I think . . . Miss Clark, to you."

"—just tell me what the hell is going on? What's that thing out there? I mean, what—"

He was babbling, and he clamped his jaws tightly, closed his eyes until they stung, knowing he sounded like a madman, the last thing he wanted when Janey herself sounded mad.

Then the headache returned in such a rush he gasped and nearly fell. "Janey, it's killing me."

"I know, poor thing. It must be terrible."

"Look, can you give me something? Something to help me? Jesus, it *hurts!*"

A patient sigh while the pain expanded, staggering him, throwing him up against the counter's rounded corner. "Oh, Jesus, it's killing me, Janey!" The heels of his hands *step-tap* pushing against his temples, grinding at the fire *step-tap* while the muscles in his neck bulged to reddened cords.

"Michael?"

"She's dead," he said. Babbling; damnit, stop babbling. "She's dead."

"Dead? Who's dead, Michael?"

"Cora. God, didn't you know that? Cora's dead, I saw her and she gave me this apple and I ate it and she's dead, she was always dead, Janey, and Jesus Christ it hurts so bad!''

"Michael?"

His eyes opened.

"Michael, do you love me?"

Something moved in the white hall.

"Janey, please, you've got to call somebody. Call the security guards, the police. There's—"

She whirled away from him, her cap spinning to the floor, and he told himself, *it's only the head-ache, only the drugs*, when he saw her eyebrows thicken, and darken, and meet over her nose while her lips pulled back in a low steady hissing and her teeth bared and sharpened while her uniform turned black.

He yelled, stumbled back, and fell against the wall. Yelled again when she lashed the chair to one side and lunged over the counter, to fall on the dark creature that sprang out of the white and met her in midflight.

"Janey!" Almost weeping. "Jesus God, Janey!"

Too afraid to move, one palm pressed against the tile, he held the crutches tightly to his chest and sidled to the right until he was stopped by the corner.

Listening to the snarling that sounded more like

thunder, the screeching that echoed in gunshots from the walls and down the hall; seeing flashes of black limbs coiling madly over black, and flashes of red that hung in the light, spattered on the counter, landed on his arm and dripped to his fingers until he wiped them off on his nightclothes with a shudder and a moan.

Listening to the sound that began as a moan and rose to a scream that made him cover his ears and press his face against the wall and kick at the baseboard with the side of his cast until there was just a silence laced only with his sobs.

His nose ran, and he wiped it with his arm.

He put a shoulder to the wall until he could lean on the crutches, move to the desk, and grab a tissue for his eyes.

The ache that burned his head had faded, had gone, and he felt as if his skull were filled now with cool air.

Migraine, he concluded as he stumbled around the counter; on top of everything else, I'm getting goddamned migraines. Which would explain the intensity of the light, and his inability to distinguish features until he was close enough to touch. But it didn't, he thought, explain the nightmare he had seen, Janey's transformation, the battle, the blood on his arm.

The hall was empty.

He swayed.

All the elevator doors were open, and there were shadows inside.

Christ, he thought, I gotta get out of here. I gotta find a doctor; I've gotta find Carolyn.

He kept to the center of the floor, not looking to the side, not listening to the husking that came from the open doors. Not bothering to call Janey because Janey was gone—if she had ever been there, if what he had wasn't ruining his mind.

His leg began aching from the pounding he gave it. The crutches bored into his armpits and hunched his shoulders to bear them. At the intersection he paused only long enough to look left, then swung into the corridor and headed toward the back, toward the place where he knew the fire exit was though its soft red letters were hidden by the white.

"I'm crazy," he said and heard the catch in his voice.

"I'm sick, that's all," and that sounded much better.

One step, one step, scraping the cast over the floor, looking into the other rooms and seeing nothing but white, hearing no voices but the rasp of his breathing, not even the smells to tell him where he was; one step, and he swerved when his left leg gave way, stiffened before he toppled and the sweat ran from his chin.

God, he thought.

"Oh, god, please help me."

Dragging the cast.

One step at a time.

Staring at the window at the far end of the hall, watching it steadily, watching it grow, not caring that all he saw was a shabby white ghost with curious wooden arms and a laughable gait and a head of wild hair that gave his skull spikes. Watching it, pacing it, once tilting his head sharply to be sure it was him, and laughing until he heard the hysterical trill and shut himself off before the scream came again.

One step, dragging; one step at a time.

Thinking about his father, hearty and loud and chasing off the night demons with a flick of his hand; thinking about his mother, slim and always grey and banishing the night creatures with a smile and a lamp.

Thinking of Cora—no! She's dead, you didn't see her.

Thinking of Rory when he reached corridor's end and looked at the fire door and knew without trying it was going to be locked.

Rory.

He had to get Rory out of this place, and nothing his fear told him could change his direction as he passed the door with a groan and rounded the corner.

On his right, an alcove lined with monitors and dials and things he'd never seen that watched the rooms across the way. There were numbers on each screen, a name taped above, and when he saw the boy's place, he moved on again, veering toward the blinded windows that looked in on the dying until he reached an open door, stopped, and looked in.

The bed was small, and Rory even smaller, his hair completely covered by a red-stained cap. Wires. Tubes. A soft-beeping tone that matched a wriggling line on a pale green screen. And no one inside, on the chair by the bed or the chair by the door.

He rapped the jamb with a crutch, not wanting to startle the kid, and when the sound died, he heard the scratching behind.

Sharp wood on tile; a nail along the wall.

"Rory," he whispered, and took a step in.

"Rory, old pal, it's me, Mike. Wake up."

Scratching, much softer, steady and sharp.

To the bed and leaning over, seeing the eyes move beneath the closed eyelids, seeing the chest rise and fall, and seeing the thin red stain on the cap stain the pillow.

"Rory," he said as he shook the boy's arm.

This time, when the pain came, he refused to admit it, widening his eyes for a clarity that was frightening, breathing slowly and deeply and feeling winter air pass over his teeth. He leaned down and touched the boy's shoulder, pushed it, pushed it harder, and turned when he heard something stop in the door.

"Michael, you should be in bed, you know."

Rory stirred, muttered something.

"Carolyn," he said, and sagged onto the bed. "My god, I'm glad to see you. I'm—" The pain; his head expanding. "God, I hurt so bad. You don't know. And I'm scared. I've got to have something, I gotta get Rory, I've got to—"

"Michael," she said, the white against her white, seemingly floating. "Michael, I do think you should go back to bed."

Scratching, intermittent and turning softer still, turning Carolyn around to put a hand to her mouth.

He was off the bed at once, swinging toward her like a sailor fresh to dry land, damning the headache, damning the pain, damning Rory, who was groaning and asking for him.

"Carolyn, listen, I've got to tell you something."

Her arm lowered and she shook her head. "Not now, Michael. Can't you see I'm busy?"

Angry, suddenly and uncontrollably angry, he grabbed her arm and turned her, pulled her close to his face so she could better see his eyes and the taut slash of his lips. "I don't give a shit if you're busy," he said, spraying her with spittle. "I am in agony, goddamnit, and we have to get the boy out of here before something else goes wrong!"

"Something else?" she said, easily pulling away.

"I'm going to kill you," he muttered. "I swear to Christ, I'm going to kill you."

The scratching was gone; the sound of wings now, and Carolyn lifted her arms, threw back her head, and he told himself it was only the pain he was seeing, only the pain that made him crazy, only the pain that lifted her slowly off the floor and turned her long hair into long shimmering feathers, turned her hands and arms into long outstretched wings, turned her face to a demon's face that spat acid on the walls and met his gaze with slanting eyes before sweeping away, out of sight.

Rory whimpered.

The pillow reddened.

Michael held onto the doorframe and watched what was Carolyn meet what was following in a slashing of claws and a slashing of beaks and a shrieking that resounded like screams against stone; a whirling, a thudding, the clear rending of flesh that splattered against the walls and made him duck back inside. Look out and see a wing lying on the floor, feebly twitching, convulsing, making him retch and pull back to see Rory lift his arms and grab for the ceiling.

where do monsters come from, Mr. Kolle?
It hurt. Dear God, it hurt.
from here, pal, in your head.
Wailing in the hall, and the crack of snapped bone, the thud of collisions and the rainsplash of blood.

No, he thought, as best he could think through the fire in his brain; and he took a step toward the bed, lost a crutch, and fell. He landed on his side, his cast striking the floor in time to his scream, the scream driving off the pain as he crawled for the footboard and pulled himself to the boy's side.

"Rory!"

Grabbing an arm and yanking, digging his nails into the wrist and yanking again.

"Rory, wake up!"

No, he thought again as he climbed onto the mattress and stared down at the boy, who was shaking, not trembling, so that the flesh of his cheeks quivered and his arms flopped about and his ankles drummed the sheet until Michael clamped them down with the weight of his legs. Then he slapped him. And again. And the skullcap seemed to bulge while the noise in the hall rose to a keening, and held there, and held, until Michael slapped the boy again and drew blood at his mouth.

And *no* a third time. Imagination wasn't real,

and monsters weren't real and a little boy in a small hospital couldn't create them just because he was afraid of what he didn't understand.

More gently: "Rory."

And there was silence in the hall.

He heard it when he heard the beeping in the room and saw the boy's shaking calm and finally end.

"Michael?" It was Janey.

"Michael?" It was Carolyn.

"I'm sorry," they said, "but you'll have to go to bed."

He looked over and saw them standing in the doorway, not changed, just as always, with a wheelchair between them and faint smiles on their lips. For a moment he couldn't move, then he looked down at Rory, who was smiling in his sleep, the bandage cap on his hair white and untorn. A finger to the boy's cheek, an apology, and he crawled off, waited for the chair to take him, and leaned back and sighed.

"Am I crazy?" he asked as they wheeled him from the room.

The white was gone, no blood, no feathers, no talons, no fangs.

"You're tired," Janey told him, leaning over to kiss his cheek. "You're not a superman, Michael. That stuff's for kids."

"But the hallucinations," he said, and tensed as he waited for the migraine to return.

"Your leg," Carolyn told him, stepping around the side to rap a hand against the cast. "You ignore the pain there and it'll cause stress and eventually find a place somewhere else. It was foolish, Michael. You're not a kid anymore."

"I want to go home," he said when they reached his own room. "I want to go home, take a bath—I don't care if I have to hang my leg over the side—get a bottle of scotch, and listen to my records. I want to—"

"No," Janey said, pursing her lips as she lifted him to the bed. Stripped off his gown and pulled another, a white one, from the bedtable drawer. "I'm sorry, Michael, but I don't think you can. Not for a while."

He lay back, then sat up. "Wait a minute."

"She's right," Carolyn said, picking up his chart and tucking it under her arm. "I think . . ." She put a finger to her lips and looked at the ceiling. "No, I think not."

"Well, why the hell not? Jesus, do you know, do you have any idea what the hell I've been through tonight? Christ, I'll be lucky to get any sleep at all here." He lifted a hand, pounded it angrily on the mattress. "First thing tomorrow, I'm checking myself out."

Carolyn shook her head.

Janey waved a *careful* finger.

"Why not?" he demanded, feeling heat on his face, feeling his heart racing. "Is it the leg? I don't have to walk. I can stay in bed there just as good as here? Medicine? Aspirin, that's all. The stuff you gave me sent me into orbit."

"Michael," Janey said sternly.

"No," he said. "I am not going to stay."

"Oh, yes you are," Carolyn said. "You'll stay until I'm good and ready to let you go."

He couldn't believe it. He'd just been in and out of hell, and they were scolding him, actually scolding him as if he'd stolen cookies from the kitchen or tied a can to the family dog. It was nuts. And he told them so, and told them further he'd be damned if he'd see either one of them again.

Janey laughed.

Carolyn laughed.

He clenched his fists and held his breath, determined not to lose the rest of his temper. "All right, then," he said when he knew he wouldn't shout. "All right, doctor, why can't I leave?"

Janey left, and he heard her still laughing, softly now but laughing.

"Doctor?" he said again, as coldly as he could.

"You can't leave because you're not finished."

"Oh, really? Not finished with what?"

"Michael," she said as if he should have known. "Honestly, Michael, when are you going to learn?"

And she switched off the light over his bed, walked out, and closed the door behind her. He gaped at the knob, the jamb, and floor, and his fists; he slapped aside the covers, and when he couldn't find the crutches, he swung his legs over and inched his way along the mattress until he reached the bottom. He waited, listened, narrowed his eyes, and counted. When he hit ten he pushed forward and caught himself against the wall.

"Not bad," he said grimly.

And opened the door.

"Oh, my god."

The white was gone, and so was all the light.

The corridor was dark, unrelievedly black, and not even his memory could tell him where he was, where the elevators were, the nurses' station, the fire exit, the opposite wall.

"Oh, my god."

Nothing but the black, and step-tap and scratching, and the flap of leathered wings and the hiss of scaled limbs and the murmuring of voices, rasping and cold.

As slowly as he could, not thinking, barely breathing, he closed the door and hugged the wall, waiting until he was sure he wouldn't ruin it by screaming.

Then he reached behind him for the bed, found it, felt it to be sure and finally climbed into it, quietly, so quietly, so he wouldn't attract them, so they wouldn't know he was here, all alone in his room.

Deep breath, he told himself; deep breath, don't panic, don't panic, you're all right.

Freezing when the sheets rustled *don't panic*, breathing through his mouth as he pulled the sheet and blanket to his chin, *don't panic you're all right*, ignoring his aching legs as he slipped down, slipped under, pulled the covers over his head and closed his eyes, and waited.

Praying for Rory to wake up, or for Janey to come and save him, or for Marc to give him a call, or for Carolyn to take him home where everything was safe and everything was fine and Jesus, Dear God, he thought as the headache returned, suppose it isn't the kid, suppose it isn't him.

And when he heard the door open, and when he felt the bed move, there was nothing more to do but open his mouth and start screaming.

Michael screaming in the dark.

And no one left to hold his hand.

Epilogue

*I*t was evening, in November, and I should have been cold.

Perhaps I was, but I held it at bay with a roll and lift of my shoulders while I watched that old man sift through the orchard like a black ghost on a black night seeking its grave. Pausing. Touching a branch, stroking a bole, putting a hand to his stomach when the coughing was too great. Looking up at the stars, at the slow rising moon, his lips moving slowly, his right foot marking time to a tune I couldn't hear.

I knew what he was doing.

He was saying goodbye.

I didn't want that, of course. I didn't want him to leave me to face the winters on my own, to walk ahead of the shadows with no one beside me, to dial his number and have no one answer but a recording that told me he wasn't there, and would not be.

I also needed him to tell me that things were still perfectly normal in the Station, the way it was everywhere else, that it was only my imagination that gave it the masque out of which stared a scream. And to be honest, I've often wondered how much of what he gave me was a wink from a New Englander to a gullible child in man's clothing.

But on the other hand, there is always that damned other hand.

Judge Alstar and his wife, for example, still live over on Raglin, and though I've shared an occasional drink with them at the Mariner Lounge, they don't talk about the nephew who some say is dead and others say has run away and still others whisper has a home in an asylum. What he does talk about is the tomb the boy made out of a block of solid wood, the promise and talent it exhibits, the uncanny way it has captured the image of a girl the boy loved and lost. He won't show it to anyone; he keeps it in the cellar.

I went to Amy Niles's funeral because she was one of the few in the village who knew my work and read it, and I was saddened by her passing and by the closed coffin at the viewing. Brett was there, too, with his second wife, Victoria, and the day after the service he handed in his resignation and they moved back to her home, someplace in Vermont.

Les, I understand, is on a scholarship at Yale.

One of my closest friends here is Callum Davidson—close because we're neighbors, and friends because we share a similar love for old and new movies, primarily the bad ones he shows late Friday nights for a group of like-minded fools who love to laugh at disasters and beautifully bad lines.

The night of the storm that knocked the power out of the village for almost eight hours he closed the theater after the first show. Two days later, Iris and Paul Lennon, the owners of Yarrow's Bookshop, advertised in the *Station Herald* for a new manager, and the day after that, Melody Records and Tapes had a new clerk behind the counter.

I shifted the papers from one hand to the other, caught a sheet as it slipped out, stuffed it back, and shook my head.

Marc and Natalie Clayton were the ones who brought me to the Station over a decade ago. I remember him telling me about this overaged kid he'd hired for the newspaper last summer, an old friend who was in need of a good boost in morale.

The day before Abe called me, I met Marc on the street and he told me that Mike Kolle had run away again. That's the way he put it, and he sighed, because Mike had been running most of his life.

Rory Castle and his pals play in my front yard now and then.

I don't know.

But I'm cold.

And I can't see Abe now, back there in the orchard, and I think I'm never going to see him again.

Nevertheless, it's still a long way back home, and I'm moving as slowly as I can in case he wants to catch up. In the dark. Under the moon. With the lights of Oxrun Station barely visible through the pines, and the crack of brittle weeds snapping under my heels, and the shadows, always the shadows, that pace at my side and whisper without words and touch without feeling.

I suspect that when I get to his house, he'll be standing in the kitchen with that bloodhound under the table and he'll grin at the surprised look on my face, point at the files he gave me, and grant me a rare laugh.

But I know that when I get there, I won't find anything at all.

He's gone; and I never said goodbye.

He's gone; and I only shook his hand.

Leaving me alone in the field, watching the stars and the moon, and listening to the sound of hoofbeats behind me, quiet and soft, listening to the *step-tap* of something moving on my left, listening to the *scratch* of something moving on my right.

And there's someone over there, standing by the brambles, the shadow of a young girl untouched by the moonlight and unruffled by the wind and reaching out her hand to give me an apple.

There's nothing to say.

All I can do is keep walking.

THE BEST IN HORROR

- [ ] 58270-5 WILDWOOD by John Farris $4.5
  58271-3 Canada $5.9
- [ ] 52760-7 THE WAITING ROOM $3.9
  52761-5 by T. M. Wright Canada $4.9
- [ ] 51762-8 MASTERS OF DARKNESS edited 3.9
  51763-6 by Dennis Etchinson Canada $4.9
- [ ] 52623-6 BLOOD HERITAGE $3.5
  52624-4 by Sheri S. Tepper Canada $4.5
- [ ] 50070-9 THE NIGHT OF THE RIPPER $3.5
  50071-7 by Robert Bloch Canada $4.5
- [ ] 52558-2 TOTENTANZ by Al Sarrantonio $3.5
  52559-0 Canada $4.5
- [ ] 58226-8 WHEN DARKNESS LOVES US $3.5
  58227-6 by Elizabeth Engstrom Canada $4.5
- [ ] 51656-7 OBSESSION by Ramsey Campbell $3.9
  51657-5 Canada $4.9
- [ ] 51850-0 MIDNIGHT edited by $2.9
  51851-9 Charles L. Grant Canada $3.5
- [ ] 52445-4 KACHINA by Kathryn Ptacek $3.9
  52446-2 Canada $4.9
- [ ] 52541-8 DEAD WHITE by Alan Ryan $3.5
  52542-6 Canada $3.9

Buy them at your local bookstore or use this handy coupon:
Clip and mail this page with your order

TOR BOOKS—Reader Service Dept.
49 W. 24 Street, 9th Floor, New York, NY 10010

Please send me the book(s) I have checked above. I am
closing $_____ (please add $1.00 to cover postage
and handling). Send check or money order only—no
C.O.D.'s.

_____

_____

_____ State/Zip _____

weeks for delivery. Prices subject to
notice.